Rose Chapman

NO JOB FOR A WOMAN

Dolly has no desire for a man in her life until a chance meeting after a church service turns her world upside down

Mereo Books

2nd Floor, 6-8 Dyer Street, Cirencester, Gloucestershire, GL7 2PF
An imprint of Memoirs Books. www.mereobooks.com
and www.memoirsbooks.co.uk

No Job for a Woman
ISBN: 978-1-86151-089-1

First published in Great Britain in 2025
by Mereo Books, an imprint of Memoirs Books.

The address for Memoirs Books can be
found at www.mereobooks.com

Mereo Books Ltd. Reg. No. 12157152

Typeset in 11/17pt Sabon
by Wiltshire Associates.
Printed and bound in Great Britain

Chapter 1

"No!"

"Well, you may as well…"

"I will not be marrying Percy Wilkins, and that is final."

Dolly Cooper was arguing with her mother, and not for the first time. Dolly, who had actually been christened Dorothy after her birth in 1896, was now 25. She had a good job. She earned good money, though not as much as the men in the factory. Even if men and women were doing exactly the same job, the men earned more, but Dolly earned more than most young women of her age, and a lot more than girls in service.

Dolly was a lathe worker in a small engineering factory making component parts for cars. During the Great War, which had ended three years before, it had been making parts for tanks and aircraft.

Dolly still lived at the family home in the village of

Oak Hill. She got on well enough with both her parents, but she had never been one to allow anyone to push her around. She knew her own mind. Though she avoided confrontation if she could, feeling it led nowhere, she stood up to her mother when it was strictly necessary.

Her mother thought she should get married. Percy Wilkins had come home safe and sound from the fighting - well, not completely sound, for he had been shot in the foot on the Somme and had lost two toes. He was now a cowman working with her dad. He was nice enough, but she had no wish to get married. She liked her independence. What was more, when she did marry she would make it clear to her spouse that she was going to stay with him by choice. So many of her relatives and friends from school days were trapped, for they relied on their man's wage to even scrape by.

"Gladys was married and had a kiddie by your age," said her mother, determined not to let the matter drop.

"Well, lucky Gladys." Gladys was Dolly's cousin. She went on, "The last time I saw her she had a short sleeved summer frock on and there were bruises all up her arm. I think he knocks her about."

Dolly could have continued to defend her decision on several fronts. She knew some men stopped off at the pub every payday and drank a chunk of their wage before even getting home. Many women had to scrape by to feed and clothe the kids, never mind themselves. She could have pointed out that they were all better off thanks to the money she put in the household kitty each week, for her father was an agricultural worker, regular wage but bottom rung of the social ladder if you discounted vagrants. But there was no point in going at it any longer with her mother.

Dolly left the room and went upstairs to the bedroom she shared with her sister Agnes. She walked to the dressing table and laid her left hand on a buttonhook that lay there. She had long fingers and her nails, which were scrupulously clean and cut straight across. Sometimes she tried buffing them to make them shine, but not often. In a way her hands showed the kind of person she was, sensitive, tidy and precise, and in touching her button hook it showed a fondness for her few nice possessions.

There were times when family members teased her, saying she was 'a lady' at heart. "I'm blest if she i'nt a throwback from some hanky-panky by one of our ancestors or summat" was how her father Bert, an agricultural worker, put it.

Dolly did not have aspirations of grandeur, but she did have flair when it came to choosing clothes, the things in which she took an interest and her phraseology when she spoke. She read her Dad's newspaper when he had finished with it. She had started reading part of his paper as soon as she had learned to read. She liked to keep abreast of what was happening in the world.

In the days when there had been the first threat of war and the Kaiser was causing trouble in Europe, she used to look towards the ceiling deep in thought after reading from the paper, but she made no comment. This was partly because her mother and sister thought a woman reading the paper was strange and for one as young as she was then, it was even more so. Newspapers were for men. The other reason she made no comment was because she did not want to sow a seed of worry in the minds of her young brothers.

Before that, at school, she had absorbed the details of the world atlas and could more or less place any country on the continent to which it belonged, though getting the many African nations in the right place was a challenge. She certainly knew about South Africa because of the Boer War, and Crimea too, where so many had been slaughtered during the war between the Russian Red Army and their White Russian opponents, was still much talked about.

Most villagers were born, schooled, employed and subsequently died without going further than the nearest town, and that only rarely, for there were village shops that fulfilled needs. Travel was not easy. People were used to walking a couple of miles to work, often along field paths or bridleways. Some had bikes. Horses were in common use, and where Dolly lived, there was a blacksmith in the village street. She loved to lean over the half open door and watch the horses being shod, though she screwed up her nose when the smell of burning hoof wafted by.

Even in this haven she knew that, should war come, it would affect them all.

Dolly's full name was Dorothy Ellen Cooper. If her parents, Bert and Beattie, had chosen to call her Ellen, no doubt it would have been changed to Nellie, another witticism of the time, based on Ellen spelt backwards. If she thought about it at all it, it never worried her. "Yes, I'm Dolly," she would now say if asked.

She was Bert's eldest child. Her dad was basically a ploughman, but he did any job round the farm, whatever his employer demanded: hedging, ditching, repairing drystone walls. He could and did turn his hand to anything. 'Demanded' is not truly a fair word, for the farm owner, William Bourne, was a just employer. The workers got Saturday afternoons and Sundays off, except during harvest when a break in the weather meant all hands out in the fields to get the harvest in, Saturday afternoon included but not on a Sunday. Sundays were sacrosanct. They were a time for church, then a walk as a family in the afternoon.

Dolly had three younger brothers, who shared a bedroom. Their home was a semi-detached 'tied' cottage that came with the job. It had an indoor cold water tap over a stone sink in the scullery, a luxury not enjoyed by everyone in the village. Many went to outside pumps to get water. There was often one pump by the road to serve a row of up to six cottages.

In their house, in addition to the scullery, there was a kitchen and a parlour, often called 'the front room'. It smelt musty and was seldom used, and Dolly only went in there when her mother sent her to water the aspidistra. As far as she was concerned she liked the warmth and muddle of the kitchen, which had armchairs as well as a table and upright chairs. Their dog and cat were allowed on the furniture. The place was clean, but her mother was not precious about possessions.

Dolly could never remember being hungry and she was always well shod. Of course, now she was working it was up to her to provide for herself, but as a child she had had good boots that fitted and enough to eat. The food was basic, but she never went to bed hungry. As for the boots, her dad had a cobbler's last, three-sided and each part of a different size, one for children's shoes and two sizes for adults. The local name for a cobbler was a 'snob'. Her dad did their snob work, putting on new soles and heels.

Some of her clothes were cast-offs from cousins, but her mother was handy with a needle and in the days when she attended school, she had a clean apron, a warm coat and clothes that fitted, even if they were much mended at elbow and wrist.

Every autumn there was a week off school for potato picking. The crop was dug up by the farmer, then women and children went into the fields to pick up the 'spuds'. The majority used the money they made to buy winter coats for the children, known in verbally handed down history in later years as the 'potato coats'. Dolly knew that in some parts of the country there were school holidays for hop picking. Families from London came out to counties such as Kent and picked hops, staying in basic accommodation on the different hop farms. The hops were then dried in tall conical buildings known as oast houses. Dolly was avid for knowledge and stored such information up. She knew that her part of England was just a piece in a national jigsaw.

In their own family what they needed they had, but frivolous possessions were not part of their world. Dolly had had a rag doll when she was six and Daisy the doll still sat on her bed. At that time her brothers would say their favourite possession was a catapult! She smiled indulgently when she thought of her brothers. Her mother was inclined to shout at them and urge her dad to "Tell them, Bert" which her dad dutifully did, but he had been young himself once and what he said was to placate their mother. Inwardly he thought they would become fine young men, not that he always approved of their shenanigans. Will, the eldest boy would go scrumming, more for bravado showing off to his mates than because he wanted the apples. Will was full of bold ideas and was always leading Lenny on.

"Our Dolly tells me a hundred years ago people were deported for stealing apples," Bert would tell him. "Watch it!" Walnut and chestnut trees grew on the village green, so they were there for the taking.

The three boys had come along a bit after Agnes and Dolly. Will was eight years younger than Dolly, and then had come Lenny and finally Jim. Once he could walk, Jim would toddle after his brothers, keen to keep up with them. Bert knew that from then on, they would let him drag along. They were really kind lads and very defensive of family. Yes, he was proud of them.

Which brings us to the button hook. Dolly could not remember where it had come from, but she had had it since she started school and learned to button up her own boots. It had a silver coloured hook, probably not real silver, and a carved handle made of mother of pearl. Dolly rather thought it had come from her great grandmother. She had always liked it. It lay on the dressing table in the bedroom she shared with her sister.

She and Agnes respected each other's things and Agnes watched and smiled whenever she saw her sister straighten the button hook or just touch it, almost like a ritual, a sign of reassurance that all was well and that would not change. Dolly touched it now. She smiled, remembering the time when a button had come off one of her boots on a Sunday and sewing it on was strictly forbidden that day. She had bawled and her mother had said, "How many times have I told you to check them on a Saturday and put a stitch or two in any wobbly ones? No you cannot do it today, nor will I do it for you. You'll have to go to church with one button off and I hope your grandmother doesn't see it or we will all cop it. Before you say any more what would the neighbours think if they heard a button had been sewn on on a Sunday? That friend of yours, May, she's a nice enough child but such a chatterer, She'd tell on you, that's for sure."

Such a long tirade, and all over a button. Dolly could never see what it had to do with 'the neighbours'. She was not a gossip and what went on with her peer group tended to wash over her head anyway. That too was a trait that helped determine her path in life. She was not a rebel but rather unaware of the opinion of others. That did not mean she was naïve or brash. Far from it.

Agnes was quiet by nature and, in the home environment, she took whatever came her way in her stride. She was the calm one in the melée of family life. She and Dolly were good friends as well as sisters.

Once Agnes had fallen and broken her arm. She had screamed, which had alerted the family. The arm was a weird shape. The local doctor said it would have to be set, and that meant a journey to the nearest hospital in the town.

Travel had been by cart. A relative, a great uncle in fact, had provided the cart and the poor child was jolted along in it to the hospital. By the time the arm was set it had been five or six hours since the accident. Dolly could remember the relief when Agnes, supported by their father, had walked back through the door. How pale she had looked, but she had recovered. Agnes refused to talk about it.

Other than that trauma, Dolly could not recall anything happening in the family that had left its mark on her memory.

Agnes was always unruffled. She would sit on her bed and ask Dolly to tell her what she had been up to. Then Agnes would giggle. She loved gossip and an insight into a world that was so unlike her own, but within the household she knew how to promote harmony and keep the family united, and she could foresee when things were getting edgy and knew exactly how to intervene. A cup of tea was a salve for everything, from her grandmother to the ructions caused by her young brothers.

Chapter 2

Dolly had interests unusual in a woman, and wisdom too, traits that had first begun to surface when she started school. Her father liked to talk to her about news items and they would lean on the fence at the end of the garden putting the world to rights, or he would get her to help tidy his shed and together they would chew the cud on the latest news.

Dolly's dad liked yakking with Dolly and spending time together when there were just the two of them, but his favourite 'thinking space' was his garden. Of an evening he would go out on his own to earth up the potatoes or run a hoe along the rows of cabbages. Growing vegetables meant fresh food and helped stretch the money he earned. Without his vegetable plot they would many a time have been unable to have vegetables with their main meal. Bones of roast chicken would be boiled up to make a broth and with onions, carrots and so on added a good stew would be cooked. His wife would throw in some pearl barley. To pad it out, chunks of bread would be used to mop up any left on the plate.

Whilst Bert was out in his vegetable plot, he would mull over thoughts of his family. For example, about the time that Dolly was due to leave school, he had looked to the future for each of his children without success. Dolly was a strange one indeed, not odd but strange in her knowledge, her interests, her desire to read and discuss the news. She would go far, that girl, he decided. He did not let his thoughts about her run on further to what 'go far' could mean. He only knew what it was to work for other people. In the old days, the days of the lords and castles which Dolly told him all about, the family might have been described as peasant stock. He could not imagine what would happen to Dolly, never mind what should happen to her, with all her fine ways. She was chatty, popular and full of knowledge, and he could give her no advice, but he thought perhaps that on leaving school he should let her have a bit of time to herself and hope she would find a path that would fulfil her dreams – not that he knew what they were. Oh, he was happy enough, but he wanted more for his children; he just could not think what 'more' might mean. Never once did he think 'going into service' was for her, although that was what most young girls did.

Agnes, pretty little Agnes who said so little, was docile

and quiet. She never caused him and his wife a moment of concern. She wouldn't say boo to a goose, so Bert felt there was no need to worry about her. She would go into service and plod on with whatever she was doing. Bert sometimes heard her giggling when she was in the bedroom with Dolly, but that was the only time she had spark.

How proud he had been when Will was born. A son! Wasn't that what all men wanted, a son and heir? He could imagine taking Will to work on the farm. He was happy enough there himself and he had no doubt Will would join him. Bert sighed. Lenny and Jim, well they were a bit young as yet. What will be will be, he thought as he put his tools away.

Dolly, and subsequently the rest of her siblings, attended the village school, starting at aged five and leaving when they were fourteen. On her first day at school Dolly had met May. They were instantly drawn to each other, and a strong friendship began.

The girls' playground was separated from the boys' by a wire fence, so they played separately: spinning yoyos, what's the time Mr. Wolf?, skipping, two-ball and so on. In class the boys and girls were mixed, often according to ability. May and Dolly used to giggle if they were sent to sit by a boy, and on the way to and from school, young as they were, they would discuss their passion for Donald Booker or Johnny Markham and so on. They were two popular girls who got on well with everyone.

It was Dolly's interest in geography that drew her closer to her father, for when they discussed what news was in his newspaper it enabled her to contribute in a mature way to their chats.

The 'top' class in school was Standard 7X. Only selected pupils were in that class. The teacher was Mr. Green, who was the headmaster at the school. Dolly was promoted to Standard 7X, while May finished her schooling in Standard 7.

"Don't worry about me, just because I'm a pea-brain," she had said to Dolly. They had laughed about it and continued as friends walking to and from school together, and when they 'got their freedom', in other words left school, they continued to take many of the next steps in life together.

From those early days it could have been assumed that Dolly would follow the usual path: get some job or other to tide her over until by eighteen she would be married, likely to one of the boys she knew from school, but it did not turn out that way. Boys and girls, men and women alike, were her friends. May was always her best friend, her confidante, but Dolly quietly deliberated over each step she would take, evaluate any decision as best she could. Apart from talking to her dad, she made her own plans. She had both the will and the determination to follow a path she chose.

Chapter 3

On leaving school Dolly had stayed at home for a while to help her mother. It was her dad's idea, a liberal thinking man. He had said, "Take a bit of time off now. You'll not get another break till you look like your grandmother, that's for sure." She liked domestic chores, did lots of cooking, but avoided helping with the washing if she could, especially when the copper was going in the outhouse boiling sheets and creating so much steam it was hard to see across the room. Agnes would get her turn in due course.

That worked well for a time, but those neighbours whose opinions bothered her mother so much commented on Dolly not earning money, saying she was relying on her father and was being idle and lazy. Dolly wondered if they said such things to her mother's face. If not, how did anyone know what the neighbours said? Who cared anyway, was Dolly's view. Some of these spiteful remarks were passed on to her by May, who would say, "That lot of old biddies! Don't take any notice."

When May had left school she had gone to work in Elliots', a department store in their local town. It was huge by local standards, but the few who had been to London knew that it in no way compared to London stores such as Derry's on Kensington High Street.

One of the disadvantages of living in a village was that everyone knew everyone, and you were related to half the other villagers anyway. That was also the advantage of living in a village, for a helping hand was usually offered when needed. In May's case her uncle was a carter and he often gave her a lift to work on his cart, at least for the first year or so. Later travel would change, nationwide.

The only thing that Dolly envied about May's job was that she got to put the customers' money in a metal box, then pull a string and it would travel to some distant office. Dolly would have liked to have a go at that, she decided, when May told her all about it.

All of which shows that in her young life Dolly was, at first hand or second hand, gaining a variety of experiences. She would churn them all over in her mind, and all, in some way or other, influenced her.

As for employment, she knew her maternal grandmother had plenty to say about Dolly being at home after leaving school. Granny did not live with them. She had an almshouse down the hill near the church, and from that short distance she tried to make the rules, or as her son-in-law put it, 'stick her oar in', when she could. These particular almshouses had been built from money provided by the Traynor family and each resident got a small sum of money each week in addition to their house. Granny had been lucky to get one.

Perhaps Dolly was influenced by what she heard, perhaps she was tired of being at home, where she had learned that domestic bliss on the long term was not for her, perhaps she wanted an income. Either way the decision, which she announced over family tea one day, was that she wanted to go out to work. She thanked her mum for all that she had been taught, thanked her dad profusely for letting her have freedom for a while (if one could call being tied to the kitchen sink freedom, though she did not say that). She told them she was ready to go out into the world, and she would look for a job. She said she was now fifteen, and that was what she had decided.

The family exchanged glances, but made no attempt to encourage or discourage her. They knew that once Dolly was decided on anything, it was best to leave her be.

Phyllis, her cousin, worked in a big house in the village for a family called Taylor.

"There's a job going with the Taylors," her mother said. "General housemaid. Phyllis would put a word in for you." Not exciting. Long hours. Poor pay. Phylis had never said anything against the Taylors. She had never said anything good about them either, come to that, but Dolly said it would do, if she could get it. It was not a 'live in' job.

Bert mentioned it to William Bourne. "Would you give her a reference, like?"

"I thought she was home helping your wife?"

"Well she is, but that can't go on. Anyways she's getting restless, wants to do something. She'll have to go into service."

William Bourne was a caring man.

"Look Bert, I know Sir Andrew Taylor, we shoot together. If, as you say, it's not live in your Dolly will come home every evening, be there to help if needed. Does she have a bike? If not I think there's an old one in the barn. You could do it up, then she would be away from home less than if she walked to and fro. It sounds OK."

"Six till five and half day off once a month and all of a Sunday. If there are people staying in the house she will have to do more, but that's the general drift."

"Our house staff live in," said Bourne. "I'll find out if you've got it right. It sounds ideal, damn lucky in fact. I'll talk to Sir Andrew. Of course his housekeeper would normally hire and fire domestic staff and no doubt his wife would be consulted, but I can at least mention it."

Bert could not thank him enough.

William Bourne's shooting friend, Sir Andrew, agreed

to tell his wife about Dolly, which he did. Who said what after that was not known, but Phyllis called in to say the housekeeper would meet Dolly.

Perhaps Dolly was able to speak up about domestic work, perhaps Sir Andrew had influence , but the outcome was that Dolly got the job, working as general housemaid for the Taylors six days a week with Sundays off plus a half day once a month.

Dolly's decision about work was never discussed at home. If her dad thought it a surprise, knowing how often he and his wife had chatted about Dolly and the way she talked, about her grand manner, her reaching standard 7X, her avid reading of the daily newspaper – none of which fitted domestic service – they kept their thoughts to themselves. Agnes, if surprised initially, bided her time and drew no conclusions. She felt 'in her bones' that the outcome would surprise them all.

One day, after Dolly had been with the Taylors for about a year, she was sent to help in the kitchen. Used to helping her mother feed seven, Dolly knew what she was about. She could stretch meat into one extra pie. She might be working for landed gentry, but money was not wasted and Dolly's ability was soon noticed by the cook. In due course the news filtered through to Lady Taylor.

Food was lavish when there were visitors but basic, though plentiful, at other times. Dolly learned to decorate cakes with icing swirls and lines, which she had never done at home. The cook, much impressed by all she did, asked the housekeeper if Dolly could spend more time in the kitchen. Phyllis, who still plodded on in the same way as when she had first started working for the Taylors, was spitefully jealous. "Silly bitch," she said at home. "I wish I had never gotten her the job in the first place."

She could not see that she and Dolly had the same opportunities, but Dolly had a willingness to work that bit harder than others, nor did she clock-watch when it came to breaks. She would forgo lunch to keep an eye on a batch of cakes in the oven. She did not seek thanks, but it was in her nature to do a job, any job, as well as possible.

Never having moved in the social realm of titled people, Dolly had no idea what was discussed over the afternoon teacups. With one little finger raised as the cup was lifted in a genteel manner to the lips, did the visitor say to the hostess, "I've got this maid who helps in the kitchen"?

It seemed impossible, but one day after Lady Taylor had been closeted briefly with the housekeeper in the housekeeper's sitting room 'below stairs', Dolly was summoned.

"Dolly, my husband's cousin, a distant cousin actually, has visitors coming to stay at Waverley, their family home."

Lady Taylor was a snob through and through, but Dolly had no reason to dislike her. Her Ladyship went on, "Waverley is a small house, not more than six bedrooms, I fear, and only about ten acres of parkland including the formal gardens by the house. They have a weekend party coming and – oh dear, this is quite out of the ordinary – they need some extra help in the kitchen. Of course I could just send you, but this has never been heard of before so I am asking, Dolly, if you would go there to live in for a week and help the cook. I just don't know how our Mrs Bragg will take it, for it seems she relies on you more and more. Of course, Sir Andrew will pay your wage as usual."

She burbled on. Lady Taylor was very kind asking Dolly if she would mind going, though the tone of her voice indicated that refusal was not an option.

Dolly was only too pleased to go. She would see somewhere else, so something a bit different. She wanted to jump at the chance, but she played her cards skilfully.

"If your Ladyship wishes, I would be pleased to help out," she said demurely.

So it was agreed. She went off to Waverley, which was owned by James Moorhouse, a mere Esquire, no title. She learned that somewhere in the kitchen there was bound to be whatever she needed, from jelly moulds to apple peelers that screwed to the scrubbed kitchen table. At the end of the week she went back to the Taylors, as a maid changing beds or as a kitchen helper kneading bread. Amenable, helpful as ever. She never talked about her trip to others in the servants' hall and, apart from mentioning it at home, where she gave minimal detail, she kept her counsel.

She never thought about the people she had seen at Waverley. Probably they would not cross her path again and anyway she had hardly emerged from the kitchen.

She was wrong. At least one of the guests had noticed her.

If Dolly was aware of Phyllis's rancour, she never responded, but it is likely she never noticed, keeping her mind on the job in hand.

Her job was not wonderful, but it was easily bearable. If there were people staying she had to 'live in', but generally she was lucky. Best of both worlds. If asked, Bert would not have said it suited his daughter. How could one say, "My Dolly has ideas above her station and being home evenings suits her. I bet it won't be long before she finds some new path to try or take up."

He knew she pulled her weight with helping her mother with the siblings. He liked her around, too. He encouraged her open thinking and ambitions when she confided in him, though he would caution, "Perhaps best not to mention that to your mother, not yet anyway." Inwardly he had thought the new position would not last, but if he was surprised that she stayed with the Taylors he made no comment.

He would never have put her into the 'obedient servant' category, although that was the world in which she had grown up, for he and all his relatives worked for the gentry. However, after a few months, she seemed embedded there and made no mention of a move.

The Taylors had two daughters who would be presented at court in due course. Owing to a death in the family the elder had had her coming-out delayed, and it now seemed likely that both girls would be 'out' in the same year. Dolly rather liked that custom for she equated 'out' to meaning on the look out for a husband, preferably one with cash and a title. But she kept such thoughts to herself.

The Taylor girls had been home schooled, but their two younger brothers were away at boarding school; it was not unusual for boys and girls to be treated differently. They kept their distance from Dolly socially, but not in a snobbish way, just appropriate for their situation. Dolly was fascinated by their clothes and the way their skirts got tighter. The hobble skirt was the latest fashion. They were brazen, according to Dolly's granny, for she had seen Julia Taylor lift hers above her ankles once when in a hurry; you could not stride out when wearing such a skirt.

The girls were some of the first in the district to begin to follow the new fashions. They had stunning hats, large with broad brims. They did not always wear boots but shoes with little heels and a bar across the instep. They had gaiters for winter weather. Dolly thought they and their lifestyle were wonderful. She labelled them in her mind as having the 'London look', though she did not know what that was.

It was not usual for ladies to chat to housemaids, but times were changing. King Edward was not as autocratic as his mother had been and King George V , whilst reputed to be a stern parent, was known to talk to common people when out in public. Perhaps nobility thought "if the king can do it so can I", perhaps the Taylor girls got used to seeing Dolly around. Either way change reached Oak Hill, and they did pass a comment or two to her in a friendly fashion.

Dolly spoke when spoken to by the Taylor girls. She was mindful to keep her place, but she had a winning smile, and perhaps it was this that encouraged Julia and Alexandra to stop and pass a word if they saw her in the hall or upstairs. Dolly was full of admiration for the two Taylor girls.

At home there was a sewing machine, a Singer with a handle to turn. Dolly got into the way of altering her clothes in an attempt to copy the styles she saw on the Taylor girls. Shortening a skirt was one of the things she did so that it just showed her ankles. Who could have guessed at that time that skirts would get shorter and the shape of dresses would change completely?

Here too her dad encouraged her. "I'll help your mother wash up. You get the machine out. Finish that bit you started."

Few men helped in the house, but Bert would wield a dishcloth or tea towel quite happily.

Dolly got out the machine. Secretly she longed to have one of the treadle models which you worked with your foot, leaving both hands free to hold the fabric. She sighed and thought 'ah, one day perhaps', but she never dwelt morosely or with any degree of envy on such things.

On a few occasions, one or other of the Taylor girls would give her a dress that they no longer wanted. "Everyone has seen it. I can't go on wearing the same old thing," said Julia one day. "Here you can have it," and she handed the dress over.

Pinks and greens were fashionable. She made use of what was cast her way and often sewed for Agnes too. There was a lot of material in the garments and she had ideas how she could alter them. One was of pale blue cotton, a break from the norm. The colour suited Dolly. She could only describe it as straight down from waist to hem. Perfect. Dolly cut off the lower part, and with a bit of juggling manage to tack the material back on below the bust. It suited her slim figure but emphasised her womanly shape to great effect. She was slim, but not shapeless. The hem she put at calf length. The spare material she kept planning to trim a hat with it.

Her dad and Agnes applauded. Her dad made flattering remarks, telling her she was a pretty as her mother. Agnes said it needed a hat to go with it.

"You aren't going into church without a hat!" echoed her mother with some asperity, "and I don't know when else you'll have occasion to wear it. I only hope your grandmother approves. All that leg showing!" But she smiled as she said it.

Beattie was always dreading conflict with her mother, although often among the various aunts, uncles and cousins, Beattie boasted about her clever daughter. Agnes, Dolly and their father exchanged glances. Dolly started to pack up the machine before taking the dress upstairs and hanging it carefully on a hanger.

She had no plans as to when she would wear this latest creation. As for the hat, Julia and Alexandra had shown her a picture in a fashion magazine of one that looked like an upturned pudding basin – a cloche, it was called, after the French word for bell. All three agreed it would never catch on, but Dolly knew that given the opportunity, she would wear one herself. She smiled, thinking of herself as a trail blazer and going to church in such a hat. Ideally it would be trimmed with a bow to match her newly revamped blue cotton dress. That would be Paris fashion, according to the magazine.

Over time her skill developed, for she acquired a sense of style. She knew what suited her, even if it deviated from the craze of the moment. She wore her outfits to church. Her Granny tutted, but Bert winked at his wife and walked beside both his daughters with pride, his portly stomach bulging, his hair slicked back in Sunday fashion and a grin on his face.

In church they sat towards the back in the rows of pews used by most parishioners. William Bourne, Sir Andrew Taylor and their families, other nobs in the village and even the residents of Waverley, when they were visiting and not at their own parish church, had pews at the front, each closed off by a low wooden door. Gentry were afforded such recognition. Dolly wondered, as she dropped her silver sixpence into the collection bag, if they were benefactors to the church or whether it was just their status that gave them such entitlement. Smiling to herself, she wondered if God listened to their prayers before those of the hoi polloi. The thought of saying such a thing to Granny made her smile all the more.

At work one morning she was on the landing, about to change the beds of visitors who had been staying for the weekend but had now left. Julia was standing there holding a pale green dress made of some silky material.

By her stance Dolly could see that she was not happy about something.

Dolly dropped a curtsey, but said nothing. If Julia spoke to her, she would reply.

"Oh, Dolly. See this?" she held out the dress. "I wore it this weekend and father says there is plenty of wear in it and he will not pay for a new one. I spent all my dress allowance weeks ago. I wore this on Saturday when George Wareham was here. I cannot wear it again and have him think I have to wear the same old thing over and again. I want him to notice me, Dolly."

Making a confidante of an employee was not usual, but Julia and her sister were used to Dolly by then. They were 'Miss Julia' and 'Miss Alexandra'. Dolly would not be any less formal, even though it was suggested, being mindful that Sir Andrew, inclined to explode in temper, would not approve if he overheard such a thing. These young ladies had few close friends of their own, never having been away to school, and they were always accompanied by their mama or a relative.

Dolly could have given a number of retorts to Julia about the rot she had just talked. If she but knew how often Dolly wore the same dress.

She smiled and said, "Let's see." She took the dress and held it up. "Alter it. Green, no perhaps a contrasting coloured ribbon with yellow dots or daisies on. That's what it needs. Sew it on in places and the dress will look different. You could casually ask... whatever you said his name was?"

"George, George Wareham."

"Well, you could ask Mr Wareham."

"Actually he's a viscount."

Dolly stood silent.

"Sorry, Dolly, the dress. What were you saying?"

"Alter it, then tell your friend you love shiny green, and perhaps he remembers the other dress you wore last time he came."

"Devious!" said Julia, laughing. "But how do I alter it?"

Dolly offered to ask May what was available in Elliot's, a shop that Julia had never known existed. The upshot was that by the end of the week Dolly had some dark ribbon with yellow dots. She showed it to Julia.

"Ideal," said Julia. "Will you sew some round the hem for me?"

There was a seamstress employed by the family who came in one afternoon a week to look after the household linen. The girls and their mother had dresses made by a modiste a fashion designer, who owned her own shop. Lady Taylor ordered what she felt the girls needed, but of late she had begun to let them have some say in the matter, their father giving them a meagre dress allowance to spend as they wished. There was no one to whom they could turn for ad hoc changes, but now here was Dolly, ready, willing, discreet, understanding and full of ideas. She was an answer to their prayers.

Dolly had an idea. She held up two lengths of the ribbon from the waist but stopped before the hem. Then she put it on one side only. It transformed the dress. It was different; it was somewhat off-beat and did not look like an 'add-on' at all.

So began Dolly's involvement with the clothes of the Taylor girls.

Lady Taylor had decided it was time the girls had more social contacts, and tennis parties were arranged. The young women who came were daughters of her friends but sometimes young men came too, brothers, cousins or more distant relatives of Lady Taylor's friends.

Julia and Alexandra were bright, sociable girls and soon had a friendship group of their own. They received invitations to tennis, or a picnic or afternoon tea. This put demands on their wardrobes, so Dolly was called in to help. In a strange way it did May a lot of good too. "I'll ask May what there is in Elliots'," was a phrase the Taylor girls often heard. Fur collars and cuffs in addition to ribbons, fancy large buttons, feathers and even lengths of material were used. Never lace, as the girls said it was what their grandmother wore. "Can you ask May?" became a well known phrase, as did "I'll ask May".

One day the girls sallied forth into Elliots' while their mama was shopping elsewhere in the town. The floor manager recognised gentry as soon as they stepped in through the door and was ready to serve them, servile manner at the ready. He went red and was cut short in his tracks when they asked for May. However, he would not jeopardise their custom to meet his own pride, so May was duly summoned.

Thereafter they often went into Elliots', and May served them. They took the goods back to Dolly to deal with. As for May, the upshot was that she got promotion and a nice pay rise to go with it. "I'm deputy manager of accessories," she told Dolly, but she laughed as she said it.

It was not exactly a mind-boggling promotion, but it was a start. May would have liked to be a buyer, one who ordered what was to be sold in the shop, or at least her part of it, but that was not likely to happen. It needed family influence of some kind to reach such giddy heights.

The girls joked about their lot in life.

"At least I'm no longer the 'gofer' at everyone's beck and call," said May. "You girl, go and get some more ribbon," she said in a haughty voice, aping her superiors exactly. They both laughed.

May knew her success was thanks to Dolly and said sincere thank-yous. "See that it continues, girl," she said to Dolly in her haughty voice again, making them both laugh even more.

Sir Andrew could be charming or bad-tempered

according to his mood. Life went along more steadily if he was absent on business or closeted in his study. Dolly thought he was fond of his children, but he was never as involved with their lives as her own father was with their family. His wife must have kept him informed about their doings.

One Monday morning workmen arrived on the main lawn of the Taylor's house. "Some plan of Sir Andrew's" was the word in the servants' hall. Much rolling, mowing and measuring followed, and within a week all was revealed. It was a croquet lawn.

Dolly was on the way to the summerhouse following orders from the housekeeper just as Sir Andrew was admiring the men's handiwork.

"You, girl!" he called out to Dolly. "What do you think you are doing on this side of the house? You're one of the domestic staff, I know. Now I remember – Dolly, the one William Bourne got me to take on." His breath came quickly and he puffed out his chest and went red in the face. Dolly, with quick thinking but also with honesty, cut across the tirade.

"I beg your pardon, Sir Andrew. The housekeeper has told me to take these two tablecloths to the summer house. They are for the tea this afternoon. That is why I am by the front lawn."

Her employer did not have the grace to apologise, but he took the wind out of her sails when he said in a reasonable tone, "You ever seen a croquet lawn? You ever played croquet?"

"No, I have never played."

"But you've seen a lawn?"

"Yes, Sir Andrew. There is one at Waverley. I saw it when I was there."

"Yes. Well that's where I got the idea, but keep that under your hat. I want my wife and daughters to think the idea came from me."

Dolly wanted to ask about the boys, but she stood silent. Perhaps when they came home for the holidays they would play too. If, however, they were like her brothers, they would be off somewhere, maybe by the river jumping off a bridge, giving the fish and frogs a scare. There was a lake in the grounds of the Taylor's house complete with punt. Perhaps that was where the Taylor lads went. If they were like her brothers, croquet would not be an attraction.

She smiled as she thought about it and from her remote position wished them much fun, for she secretly thought Julia and Alexandra were too constrained. Who knew if she would rebel herself, were she put in such a position? She liked to think so.

"What are you grinning at?" Sir Andrew's voice cut across her thoughts.

"I am not grinning sir, just smiling. I was thinking how much pleasure this will give your family."

Her reply was true, even if the scenario that had given rise to her thoughts was not explained.

Sir Andrew picked up a mallet and tossed it to her. She caught it in one hand. He rolled a ball in her direction, then, with his own mallet ready, put one foot either side of a ball and swung the mallet, hitting the ball towards a hoop.

"Trick is not to move your head and look up until you have taken your shot."

He indicated that she should try. She glanced around nervously, doubtful that he would speak up for her if anyone appeared, but she need not have worried. Gingerly she put the tablecloths on the lawn and took her shot. The ball narrowly missed the hoop. She dropped the mallet and picked up the cloths, heading at speed for the summerhouse. It unnerved her, this deviation from the norm. Life was easier when everyone had a place in the hierarchy and stuck to it.

Chapter 4

Bert Cooper was quiet, and clearly not his usual jovial self. Dolly noticed this, but no one else seemed to. She had seen him leaning on a hoe in his veg plot staring into space.

"You OK Dad?" she asked him. She was leaning over the fence watching the young calves, who were skittish and jumping about, having just been let out to pasture after weeks in the barn.

"Yes. No... I'm not ill, Dolly. Don't worry."

"Dad!" she said in a tone that meant 'don't fob me off'.

"It's work. Old Billy Bourne. He's talking about hooking up with one or two other farms, running them together like. He's dropped a hint or two. I don't like it, Dolly. Will it mean farm workers losing their jobs? Will it mean I'm out? This house is tied to the job. Where would we live? If I found a cottage to rent, how would we pay the rent if I've no job? If I'm laid off others will be too, and there will be men like me looking for work."

She replied in a voice of surprise, "Billy Bourne? I've never heard you call him that before."

"Well, we do call him that behind his back like, plus a lot of words I'll not say in front of you or your mother."

"Would you say them in front of Granny?"

Bert had to smile. "She's not as innocent as she seems. Your grandfather was a drayman and he had some ripe language, as I know well enough. Bloody old bugger, Billy Bourne, that's him when he is in a 'get it done yesterday' mood. He's a funny chap, our Dolly. He never swears or raises his voice or loses his temper but he gets in a do this, do that mood and we are damned if we do and damned if we don't. That's when we let off steam by calling him Billy Bourne plus the rest, not in his hearing.

"Keep it to yourself, girl. It doesn't happen often and it is really only those of us who have worked with him, no *for* him, for years that get it. This change in his moods. He picks on us old hands, as in those who have worked for him for years. I've noticed it before. It's as though he wants us out and new young blood in, but on the other hand, he asks us what we think and he has even been known to listen to what we tell 'im, though I can't think of any time when he has changed tack because of something we said. No, our Dolly. We are labourers. That's how it is. Old man Taylor would sack you as soon as look at you. The gentry. Huh! No respect for us. Truth is, I can't sleep for worrying."

Bert was such a gentle man, always seeing the best in everyone, or at least that was how it came over to his family.

Dolly was flummoxed. "What does Mum think?"

"I knew I shouldn't have told you, Dolly. You'll go to your mother and she'll blab to your grandmother and all hell will be let loose." He was obviously letting his imagination run away with him. Dolly was furious.

"Dad! Dad! How dare you think I'd repeat anything you said!" She started to walk away, but he clutched her arm saying, "Sorry Dolly. I just can't think straight. It's really getting to me."

In another attempt to cheer him up she joked, "We could all move in with Granny." Bert clutched his chest. She was scared, thinking he was having a heart attack. He leant on the fence. His colour was good and he smiled.

"It's no joke, my girl." He turned towards the house bringing their chat to an end. That was not like him.

The next Friday evening Bert said he would take the dog out, a thing he never did, for the dog ran around the farm at will and had never had regular walks as townsfolk did with their dogs. If his wife was surprised she said nothing, and Dolly said she would go too.

"Tell all," she urged him. "What are the plans as far as you know?"

Many a farmer or smallholder got by on a few acres. The wives kept chicken, perhaps two dozen, and the eggs were sold. There would be a few sheep and a couple of calves being fed up to maturity ending at the butcher's. Sometimes there would be a gaggle of geese being fattened up for the Christmas market. Both small holders and householders kept a pig or two.

There was a range from these smallholdings to big farms of fifty acres or more. Now William Bourne was talking about linking with others so that say one hundred and fifty acres would be run together. A thousand acres had been mentioned, but Bert thought he had misheard. Impossible to imagine.

"He reckons," explained Bert, "that four teams of horses in one field ploughing would get the job done. Grab suitable weather conditions. Then move on. Maximum use of ploughs. Thatchers could cover several farms thatching hay ricks and doing roofs too. Can't see it myself. There's a new threshing machine up in the yard and a cart bought in from Sussex. Huge. Bourne says it will go farm to farm and they'll all be better off. Same with sheep shearing and dipping. One team would cover a group of farms, a co-operative of farms he's calling it. Then there's them new tractors. They cost I don't know what, so he says one or two for use over his group of farms would save wages, less workers see. It's a different way of life and we're going to be trampled underfoot, girl, underfoot.".

"Sounds exciting. Could I come and see it, the new cart and a tractor if it's come already? I'll ask Mr. Bourne myself if you like."

Bert jumped down her throat immediately. "You'll do no such thing! You keep out of it, girl."

Dolly got one afternoon a month off work. The next time it happened, Dolly, purely by chance, wandered up to the yard. Bert was not there, but William Bourne was.

"Hello Mr. Bourne. Dad was telling me about this new cart, a Sussex one he said. I didn't believe him, about its size, I mean. I hope you don't mind but I came to have a look for myself. Dad doesn't know I am here. Is it allowed, Mr. Bourne, my being here?"

Willim Bourne had no children of his own and he often spoke of a nephew, Ewan. Dolly had never seen him, though he must have been in church from time to time when he visited Oak Hill.

Mr Bourne did not answer but turned his head and shouted, "Ewan!" He had a deep voice and it echoed round the yard. A young man appeared, tall, dark-haired and broad of shoulder.

"Yes, Uncle?"

"Young woman here wants to see the new cart. May

as well show her the tractor that came today too." He turned to Dolly, "You're Bert's girl, I think. This'll stun you. Mind you, I don't know nothin' compared to my nevvy here." He left.

Ewan and Dolly looked at each other for a moment. Then Ewan spoke.

"The tractor's round here. The cart's in one of the permanent grass fields. You're interested then?"

"I did not come to waste your time, Mr...?"

"Call me Ewan. My name's Ewan Fletcher. My mother is William Bourne's sister. This way."

He did not have to give her so much information. By his tone she decided he was bored, but determined to be tolerant and do as he was bid.

He stopped beside a tractor. She had never seen one other than in advertisements. It had a seat for one man. There was no hood or roof and it crossed her mind that the driver would get mighty cold just sitting still on it.

He showed her the engine and then how other implements could be hooked on, such as their latest thresher. He talked of binders as well as ploughing. His voice changed. He said it would be used a-plenty. His words fell over themselves, so great was his enthusiasm. She knew her brothers would love to stand as close to a new-fangled tractor as she now was, but she had no wish to be too pushy and ask if they might come to see it. She should, after all, not have been there right now.

Ewan had a captive audience. She asked how he got his ideas. She learned that he had been to an agricultural college called Harper Adams. It had not been open long and, in his view, it was encouraging new ways of farming.

They moved on to see the Sussex cart.

"Been about for years, of course, but this is a gurt big thing, just what we need. It's summat, isn't it?" he asked, running a hand along the side. She was amused that he had the rural accent while his Uncle seldom lapsed into the local vernacular. He talked on about digging up permanent pasture. Some crops, like beans, would be ploughed in to put food in the soil, plant food. She tried to remember the word he used: nitrogen.

No wonder her dad was worried. This all seemed to belong far into the future.

She made her excuses and said 'Thank you'. As she left Ewan called out, "Say hello to Agnes for me."

She had seen so much that she forgot his last sentence until much later, when she wondered how he knew her sister. Agnes had never mentioned him. Of course she could ask her, but that would mean letting on that she had been up to the farm poking her nose in. She decided to keep quiet.

What she did realise was that nothing had been said about laying off labourers. Would all this change in fact generate more work? Whilst walking home she let her mind wander. Her brothers would be able to learn how a tractor worked. They could perhaps work in a garage repairing or maintaining them, or in a blacksmith's mending broken parts.

Then there were cars. They did not mean any loss of employment, but they did mean that if the old guard, like her dad, moved with the times on the farm instead of shouting and swearing about change, the new generation would find employment, but sons would not follow 'dear old Dad'.

Whenever she saw Ewan Fletcher after that, he would wave. When coming out of church he would come across and say hello. She noticed that he gravitated to Agnes and, by the look of them, they had plenty to say to each other. She thought little about it, for Agnes was not yet fourteen.

So how did Ewan Fletcher know Agnes? It had been expected that her sister would have a few weeks at home once she left school. Perhaps not as long as Dolly had.

One day, when Agnes was approaching fourteen, she stood in the garden waiting for Dolly to come home. She knew Dolly would take her bike into the shed, and she wanted a quiet word. Dolly had done well at school. She remembered being in standard 7X, made up of selected pupils only. Their classroom was the school hall and Mr. Green, the Headmaster, taught this class himself. That was still so when Agnes was thirteen, rising fourteen. The pupils had to be trusted to get on with their tasks when Mr. Green was called into the office. In all likelihood it was Dolly's geography and world knowledge gained from reading newspapers that had got her into 7X.

May had stayed in Standard 7. "Peabrain. That's me," she would joke. May was literate but not beyond average. She was also quite quiet in school, not drawing attention to herself, so she was overlooked rather than incapable and did not get to the class she called 'the brainy lot'.

Agnes was bright. She had progressed to Mr. Green's class. She loved arithmetic and Mr. Green spoke of mathematics, for they had long since progressed beyond twelve pennies make a shilling or twenty-two yards make a chain. He took pleasure in teaching Agnes and some of the boys who showed great promise. It was a subject at which he had excelled at school. He taught them a bit about book-keeping. Perhaps the boys would end up in offices.

The school was heated by big black pot-bellied stoves run on coal, one in each classroom, and when the cost went up he explained to his mathematics group, through analogy, how the money had to be found from the school's budget. When the vicar came on his weekly visit to check the registers they would go into Mr. Green's office , talking school business, he told his best pupils.

On this particular day, Agnes followed Dolly into the shed.

"Dolly, I shall leave school soon."

"And you'll get your time helping Mum. Sort of extended holiday, Agnes."

"Yes, but I don't want that. I don't like helping at home."

"But you are so good at it. Mum relies on you, and so do I."

"No, Dolly. Think carefully. I make endless pots of tea. I know how to calm everyone down. I know how to appear helpful, but I don't really do much."

Agnes had an autumn birthday.

"I want to stay on at school at least until Christmas and then start work," she said. Many left school on their fourteenth birthday and some while they were still thirteen.

"I've asked Mr. Green if I could become a pupil teacher with the infants. It wouldn't be a paid job. I'm going to tell Mum and Dad over tea, but I want to know what you think and if you will back me up against Mum and Dad."

As soon as they were all seated, Agnes began. She might have let us eat first, thought Dolly.

"I want to stay on at school and be a student teacher in the infants", she blurted out.

Bert sprang to his feet and shouted, "Well bug..."

"Bert!" interrupted his wife, nodding her head towards the boys.

Bert sat down.

"Well... bother me. I thought you loved home. What brought this on?"

"I do love home, but this is what I want to do. Sort of instead of staying to help Mum, as Dolly did."

Silence.

Bert, as though thinking aloud, started mumbling. "There's our Dolly, got into standard 7X and she's a skivvy in some household. I had never thought that would be enough for her, and now you."

"I got to 7X too Dad. Mr. Green says I can keep going to his book-keeping class as well as work with the infants." Bert felt guilty that he had had no idea Agnes was in 7X. She was so quiet she got overlooked.

Again, a silence.

"Well... if that's what you want. Till Christmas you say?"

The boys kept their heads down thinking there would be an explosion at any moment, but it did not come. Dolly had no need to say anything. Bert just sagged in his seat as though his whole body was deflating.

"So..." He had neither agreed nor disagreed, but the next day, Agnes asked Mr. Green when she could start. He was delighted. He said the arrangement could be flexible and she could continue with his extended mathematics class twice a week. He started setting homework for his 'expert' mathematicians and the whole group sped ahead, to his delight and theirs. Their parents, if they paid attention, and most did not, had no understanding of what it was all about anyway. Agnes just talked at home about the infants.

Junior and senior boys learned gardening and plots were provided in a field next to the school by the generosity of the landowner. The girls learned sewing and cooking, the latter being taught by Mrs. Green, the Headmaster's wife, in her kitchen in the school house which was joined to the school; basic things like biscuits and scones.

Agnes was grieved by some of the things she saw in the 'babies' class. In bad weather several would be absent. They came from outlying farms and dwellings and a message would be sent to say they had no waterproof boots so could not come to school along the tracks because of the deep mud. Mr. Green knew all about this, and it was only too true. Agnes wondered if William Bourne would have offered help if any of his tenants had been in the same situation. She had no idea who owned the farms the destitute people came from, or whether they were smallholders grubbing around for a few pence to survive. It was all so awful.

In their own home there was always a Christmas tree. What fun they had had each year making paper chains from long strips of paper looped together and used to decorate the house and the tree. Her mother made the glue from flour and boiling water. They had cut out paper snowflake shapes and put these on the tree too. Now that she and Dolly were 'grown up', or so they thought, just their brothers made the decorations. It all generated excitement over Christmas.

Dolly came home one day talking about the fudge that was made in the Taylors' kitchen. What a treat that would be for each of her infant class, thought Alice. One piece or even two as a Christmas present given out at a party in school when they could play Hunt the Thimble and other party games.

Mr Green was a forward-thinking headmaster. He had not been in the job long and was quite young himself. He could see the world was changing and he wanted his pupils to know what options there were out in the big wide world. He began asking people to come into school to talk about their jobs. May, for one, came to tell the girls what it was like working in a shop. Mr. Green had contacted Elliots' himself to get her the time off.

Tractors were a major topic of discussion in the boys' playground, so he asked William Bourne if there was any chance of his older pupils seeing one. The upshot was that Ewan Fletcher drove theirs down one afternoon. 7X and 7 stood round it in School Lane and Ewan did the talking. Each boy in turn was allowed to sit on the driver's seat. Girls were not invited, but no one seemed to mind. Agnes had come out with her 'babies' at the end of the afternoon and they had stood in awe. It was then that Agnes first met Ewan.

"Your little ones were very good. They just watched," he said.

"Yes, they are sweeties. I don't think they really knew what it was all about. The books in school have horses on farms. I don't think there is one with a tractor picture. Still, they'll catch on. It was very kind of you to come, Ewan – I mean, Mr. Fletcher."

"No, call me Ewan. You're welcome, Agnes."

He had started up his tractor and driven away with the smell of exhaust fumes lingering in the air. Thereafter he waved whenever he passed Agnes.

One very special day, at least in the eyes of pupils at Oak Hill school, he drove up in a motor car. Some bold boy had left his desk and looked through the window to see if the noise was what he thought it was. "A car!" he had hissed, and en masse 7X had rushed to the window.

"Ladies and gentlemen, please," said Mr. Green calmly. "This is my special surprise for you all. Mr Fletcher has brought his car for you to see." They went outside in orderly fashion and Ewan explained the workings, gear lever, brake and so on. He then let everyone sit in the driver's and passenger seats and touch whatever they wished. By the end there were sticky finger marks on doors, lights, windows and the bonnet.

Ewan left. On his way home later he saw Agnes coming out of the school gate wiping her eyes. She had clearly been crying. He stopped the car.

"Agnes?"

She looked up and tried to smile.

"Hello."

He jumped down and asked her what was up. She would not normally have answered but she was so uptight that her worries just tumbled out.

"Our Dolly has been talking about fudge. They've been making it in the kitchen where she works. She's a maid. I'd just love for my infants to have a piece of fudge each for Christmas. Do you know, today two of them had no dinner with them? Nothing at all. Not even bread and dripping. They are so sweet. If they were your uncle's tenants would he make sure they had enough to feed their children? Would he, Ewan?"

"Are they my uncle's tenants?"

"I don't know. Not all. Well, just some I think. I don't know about most."

"What would you need for fudge?"

"Sugar, cream, butter, tinned condensed milk. I've never made any, but that's what our Dolly says. Even one piece each would cost."

"What about Mrs Green?"

"I can't ask her. I mean she lets us use her kitchen. Perhaps she gives the flour and so on that we use for the things we do make or perhaps it's paid from school funds, I don't know, but I dare not ask for expensive things.

Why, we've never even had tinned condensed milk in our house."

She sniffed, looked up and tried to smile.

"Hold your horses, Agnes. No promises mind, but give me time to think about it."

So the idea was shelved.

Meanwhile Dolly chattered at work about Agnes wanting a treat for the infants. Just as she was saying this, Lady Taylor came into the kitchen.

"What's that, Dolly?" she asked. Dolly explained. Lady Taylor turned and left, but she was back in a few minutes.

"Sir Andrew will donate whatever sugar you need. I suggest you go for two or three pieces per child. May as well make it worth while if your sister is bothering." She leant towards Dolly and in a low voice said, "My husband is not a generous man. His offer took me by surprise. I expect cook has some vanilla if you asked her." She touched Dolly's arm lightly and turned to talk to Cook about weekend menus.

Just two days later Ewan pulled up in his motor car as Agnes walked down school lane.

"Hop in," he said.

"Whatever for? And no I can't ride with you."

"Business meeting with my Uncle. Up you hop," and he came round to help her into the seat next to his.

"What will people say?" Agnes was scandalised.

"Don't know. Wish we could both hear them. Give us a laugh, Agnes. Do get in. Here, put this on and tie the scarf tight or your hair will get all blown about."

He handed her a floppy straw hat with a big wide scarf to tie it in place. She put it on and climbed in. She did not know whether to look around and hope people noticed her or hang her head and try to look as though she was not aboard.

They went so fast, twenty miles an hour, and she felt wildly excited. She sat up, looked round and laughed, enjoying the wind in her hair.

They pulled up by William Bourne's farm office.

"You have a lovely smile, Agnes," said Ewan.

"Why am I here?"

Ewan laughed. "If you want stuff for fudge you'll have to ask my uncle yourself. It was his idea."

Agnes trembled, but then she thought of her tinies and the treat, so she took off the hat, straightened her hair and walked boldly into the office. Mr. Bourne stood up as she came in. No one had ever extended her such a courtesy before and she felt like royalty.

He pointed to a chair. When they were both seated he said, "Fudge. My nephew has talked about fudge. Tell me what you want and I may, may I say, help."

She explained clearly and concisely.

"I'll give whatever butter and cream you need. There's plenty here on the farm. Just tell Ewan what you want and when." He stood up to shake her hand, another first, for she was just a young girl. "Tell Ewan I've said yes and he'll take it from here."

Agnes told Ewan she would prefer to walk home, thinking, but not saying, that she had no wish to attract attention to herself. There was a spring in her step. Over tea she explained all. Her mother said she would pay for one tin of condensed milk. Dolly offered another and Mr. Green said the school budget would run to a tin if it was needed. When Julia and Alexandra heard of the project they offered to buy ribbon through May, so a real bow could be put on each gift.

After church on the Sunday, Ewan came across to the Cooper family.

"Agnes" he said, touching her lightly on the arm as he turned to her. "I've been thinking. You'll need some paper to wrap up the fudge. I can only think of tissue paper, but I'll ask Uncle's cook for ideas and I'll get it for you." She smiled and thanked him in a practical, calm way; by no means was she effusive.

By now the plan was for each child in the infant class to have several pieces of fudge each. Mrs. Green was to make it and, surprisingly with so many people involved, it still remained a secret. Fortunately Agnes's brothers were not of an age to be in her class.

"Is that all?" Ewan asked.

"A tree for the classroom would be nice, "said Agnes.

"We always have a tree at home. We could make the decorations in school. I don't think many of them have a tree at home."

Ewan leant towards her and spoke in a low voice. "You're an expensive girl to know." Then he stepped back and smiled.

"I'll get you a tree. I'll deliver it on the new tractor. How would that be?"

Agnes blushed.

Ewan's conversation with Agnes after Sunday service raised eyebrows, starting with Granny, who had noted how he leant forward at one point. To Agnes he was quite an old man. He was eight years older than her. But it was worth it. Her 'babies' would get to taste fudge.

At the infant class Christmas party each child had a piece of fudge and then some to take home. How it would be shared out when some families had ten or more children Agnes did not know, but from the school's point of view it was a great success.

Chapter 5

Every other Saturday, there was a dance in the local village hall. The music was provided by a violinist, a pianist and a double bass player. When May and Dolly were rising sixteen they wanted to start going to the dances. Bert taught the two girls how to waltz and dance the Valeta. May knew how to quickstep and foxtrot, after a fashion, so, with basic knowledge learned from practising at home to records played on a wind-up gramophone, they talked their parents into letting them go to the village hop.

"You must leave at ten, mind," said Bert. "You're both very young, even if you are now out to work."

The dances finished at eleven anyway, but they obeyed. They laughed a lot and got to dance with boys they had known at school, Johnny Markham and Donald Booker, plus some older lads they also knew from the village. It was fun. Little did they realise that before long the lads would be enlisting, and even if the hops continued, the girls would be having to dance with each other.

Popular as ever, Dolly and May had plenty of partners and enjoyed themselves. The violinist was also the organist from church. He was suffering from arthritis and his fingers were no longer as flexible as they had been. He did not want to give up playing, but he knew his time was limited.

Once Dolly and May had turned sixteen they were allowed to stay until the dance closed at eleven. It was around this time that a new violinist took up the post on a voluntary basis. He was tall and dark-haired and had a cultured voice, but he did not carry himself well and walked with a slight stoop, almost as though he was ashamed of his height and his thin figure. The girls guessed he was in his mid-twenties, but he had a solemn manner which gave him the air of an older man. Little was known about him except that he was lodging in the village. Rumour had it that he worked at New Medic, an experimental laboratory investigating new medicines. It was all very hush-hush. If he was working there it was assumed that he must be clever, a scientist of some kind perhaps.

Sometimes he left his post as violinist at the dances to take a partner and quick step around. He asked May to dance and she fell in love with him at once. Dolly got fed up with hearing about it.

"His name's Cyril," said May. "And isn't he just so handsome!"

The weeks went by. Cyril danced with different partners, but it soon became obvious that he had his eye on May and before long he was dancing only with her.

"He's coming to tea to our house, on Sunday," May said as they walked home. "Mum and Dad will just love him."

This brought change for Dolly. She was not upset, far from it; she was pleased for her friend. It had been bound to happen some time. Dolly had no interest in any of the men she knew or met at the dance. They were nice, nothing more; a bland word meaning, who would give them a second glance?

The two girls were nearing seventeen when Cyril started walking them both home. They dropped Dolly off by her gate, then doubled back down the lane to May's. Dolly did not May's door bang just after she had left them so she guessed, quite rightly, that Cyril and May were canoodling, enjoying a goodnight kiss – or ten kisses – before May went inside.

Dolly smiled; she was not jealous. She had no wish to be in such a situation. She had the world to explore. She had much living still to do before she would think of 'settling down'.

The family continued to go to Matins each Sunday,

at St Andrew's, the village Church of England church. Sermons were often tedious and pointless in her view and she got in the habit of not listening, instead escaping into her imagination. She loved getting ready for church. She had saved up to buy some shoes in modern style.

On a sunny Easter Sunday she put on a pale blue dress and a 'pudding basin' or cloche hat that she had made herself, getting the idea from a magazine Alexandra Taylor had shown her a while back. Feeling she looked the bee's knees, she walked up the path holding her dad's arm. Agnes too was looking smart, in a navy dress designed by Dolly but really a cast-off. They kissed their grandmother when they saw her. Having looked at her granddaughters, she made no comment. Even if she thought they were perfect, it was in her nature to find something to snort about.

She walked into church with her daughter. Dolly's young brothers had polished boots and stiff collars with which they constantly fidgeted. Their father seemed not to notice, to his wife's annoyance.

After the service the rector shook hands with people as they left. Many lingered chatting to each other. Dolly had got into the way of walking round the tombstones or sitting on a bench on the north side of the church. On this particular Sunday she was still with family when a handsome young man came up to her.

"Excuse me. You are Dolly aren't you? We met at Waverley." He had a deep voice, and an accent that proclaimed a public school education.

Dolly stared. She had no recollection of him.

"Sorry, I was just there helping out. I think you have the wrong person. I'm just a maid."

"You decorated a birthday cake for me. There was a croquet party and you brought it out."

Dolly was starting to back away. "Please don't go," said the young man.

For one of the few times in her life, Dolly was thrown off balance. She shook her head and walked towards the corner of the church. He followed. She glanced round. Had anyone seen? What would people say?

"Sorry, I should have introduced myself," said the young man. "My name is Peter, Peter Brunnick. I just wanted to thank you for the cake. I'm back at Waverley at the moment. Lovely relatives, but no one under sixty to talk to. I was hoping you might rescue me from my plight."

Of course, this was all very unconventional, but Dolly hesitated. He laughed and said, "Talk to me, I dare you! I promise you are quite safe."

This was beyond her. She had to smile, so she gave in and they chatted.

By this time she had reached the bench on the north side of the church. She sat back down and he sat next to her, but not too close. They began to chat, and she told him about her life and the Saturday dances. He spoke a little about Waverley and, when asked, said the croquet was a success and he liked the game.

The next Saturday, about half an hour after the dance started, in came Peter Brunnick. He watched the dancing for a while, then asked her for a dance. He did not monopolise her on that occasion and left before the end. That was just the start, for thereafter he came regularly and was soon her frequent partner. Even in a Paul Jones he managed to end up in front of her.

Hearing about May and Cyril, Mr Brunnick started walking her home. "Just for them, you understand, so they can walk together and you don't have to play the gooseberry."

There was nothing in it. His relatives owned Waverley. One part of her mind was saying, "So what?", but another could not stop thinking about him.

On the way to the dance one week, May burst out with, "My Cyril will be in church on Sunday." Dolly sighed. So what? May was besotted with Cyril, but the news that he was coming to church meant nothing to Dolly.

On the Sunday Dolly saw May and her family come in; no Cyril. But when the organ started up, in came the processional entry of the choir followed by the rector, and with him was Cyril. Dolly wondered what he was doing with the procession.

When it was the time for the sermon the Rector welcomed Cyril, explained that he was training as a Methodist Minister. There was a Methodist chapel in the village. Cyril had been invited to give the sermon at St Andrew's that day. May turned and raised her hand in a discreet wave to Dolly.

When Cyril stepped up to give the sermon, Dolly, for once, paid attention to the service. She liked the content and appreciated his clear, enthusiastic delivery. When the service was over Cyril stood by the door as everyone left and shook hands, chatting to everyone as they passed.

On the Monday May called at Dolly's house, which was unusual in itself.

"I know what you're thinking," she said to Dolly. "I was a pea-brain at school, so how come I am with Cyril? Yes, he might drop me. It's a chance I'm prepared to take, but it's worth it to get one more hour, one more walk, one more evening with him. If he disappears tomorrow I shall still think it was worth it.

"He has taught me a lot about music. Yesterday he brought his viola and played to us all. I would be happy to just hold his hand and say nothing for hours. So long as he is with me. It's a strange feeling. Anyway, I've got next Saturday off and we are going to Guildford to meet his parents. If war comes he will finish his training and then he will join the army as a padre. He wants to work with people who are in an emotional mess through war. He has met some old stagers from the Boer War.

"One thing I know will make you mad," said May. "He has some sympathy for conscientious objectors."

"Is he one?" asked Dolly sharply.

"Oh no, he just understands their point of view."

"That's all right then. Anyway, I have never really talked to him about things like that. It's nothing to do with me."

"I just wanted you to know. Don't let us fall out over this, Dolly."

"I think another war could be coming, May. He could get called up."

"Yes he could be sent to fight, but he wants to work in hospitals here as an army padre. Of course he can ask for a posting, but we both know he will go where he is sent."

"It'll lead to heartache, May. Couldn't you get out now?"

"If he asks me to marry him I will, and I'll go where he goes if possible."

The friends hugged.

"Your turn will come, Dolly. You will understand what it means to have one man as your star, your sun."

The papers were full of gloom. The Kaiser was demanding this and that. Dolly and her dad still shared his newspaper, but they never discussed anything over family tea. Few were those who did not know war was coming.

Peter was not at every dance. Dolly learned that he lived in Tewkesbury and worked in a flour mill. In a way they were now 'walking out', for after Sunday service they would sit on the original bench, or under the Lychgate, or stroll down the village street. She never invited him to her home.

As far as Dolly could understand, the mill of which he spoke belonged to his father. He obviously returned home during the week and she thought his relatives at Waverley were kind to have him as often as they did. Once or twice, when the Village Hall was smoky from all the Woodbines the men smoked, he would make excuses and go outside for a breath of air. She never took much notice. It did not occur to her that he had a health problem.

They talked of hobbies, and Peter said he liked to write poetry, which surprised her. It seemed there was a group in west Gloucestershire called the Dymock Poets. He went to ad hoc meetings with them, where they listened to parts of poems being written. He was very moved by some, those by Rupert Brooke in particular.

"In some corner of a foreign field there is for ever England," he quoted. "A bit like Hardy's Hodge, the drummer *beneath some southern tree.*" She loved the way he talked. She loved the fact that he had an unusual hobby. The poems had not all been published as yet; it

was more an exchange of ideas. What he did say was that everyone believed war was coming. Some poems were about nature, to remind soldiers of the English countryside. He mentioned a few names of members: Masefield, Gibson, Frost. There were others. No he was not a member just an invited visitor. He then went on to say he felt so full of energy when out in the forest away from the flour mill. If only he could live there.

Chapter 6

The Coopers were all pleased for Agnes and her success with the infant class at Christmas. Bert and his wife thought she would then look for a job, but she announced over tea that she wanted to stay on as a student teacher. She had grown up a lot in a short time. She no longer sought support from Dolly before saying anything to her family. Bert would have said she grew more like Dolly, with wilful ideas. She had set herself a path that she was determined to follow.

Ewan continued to visit the village school, and it was not long before her young brothers began to boast about seeing a car or sitting on a tractor. He was a hit with the children. As for the advanced mathematics class, Ewan, with his uncle's permission, gave some talks on cost of animal feed, buying in seed, sheep dip or auctioneers' percentage gain at cattle markets. Agnes lapped it up.

Mr. Green set up mock book-keeping, using hypothetical figures.

She did love helping with the infants. What she did not admit to anyone was the fact that she wanted to join the commercial world, which was almost unknown for a woman, at least out here in the country. She said that, if necessary, she would find a means of continuing to attend Mr. Green's mathematics classes. She did every bit of homework set, and made no errors in calculations.

Her success at Christmas helped her make the decision to stay on as a student teacher, at least until the long summer break. Mr. Green said the budget would run to a salary, which would be about the same as she would get in service, but it would not include a uniform or her keep, so she would be poorer than a kitchen maid in a big house.

She made her announcement over family tea. If her parents were surprised, they resorted to saying, "Well, if that is what you want," and did not oppose her.

Did the Coopers talk other than over family tea? Of course. In the privacy of their bedroom Dolly and Agnes decided over the years that they had twigged that major announcements made at such a time met with least resistance, their parents not wishing to bring the boys into any family row. Either way the girls usually got what they wanted.

Agnes stayed on at school. She often saw Ewan there and grew bold enough to go for a drive with him in his car. They could talk non-stop and had many a laugh too, but she still saw him as relatively old, and of course out of her social class.

One day talk turned to motor charabancs owned by a local firm. They made trips to the seaside. Agnes was in awe and chatted to Ewan.

"I'll take you in my car, if you like," he said.

"Would it go that far?"

He put one hand on his chest and pulled a face of mock hurt.

"I am so upset! Cars drive from London to Brighton and you ask if my car could get to the sea. Yes, of course." He tapped the steering wheel and said, "Jemima here is perfect."

In fact they never did take the trip. Ewan was busy setting up the multi-farm group. He worked long hours. Some of his work was on other local farms, part of the new conglomerate, but he also travelled nationwide to see innovations in action.

He came back from one trip saying it was essential to have an office with a manager who knew about farming. There was a draughty room in the stable block that William Bourne used, but this was to go and the old dairy was to be extended and a new office created. A telephone would be installed there, plus several desks. A separate room for the boss and visiting important persons would be provided. Financial control with dual-entry book keeping would be set up.

Agnes was now nearing fifteen. The long school holidays were in sight and it would be a good time to change jobs, if – and it was a big if – she could get into an office. She pricked up her ears. Now was the time to jump. She could be a book-keeper. She knew she could succeed if someone gave her a chance. Who to approach, when and how?

Mr. Green was her first port of call. He agreed to support her application, which was bold of him, for he knew there would be gossip about his pupil teacher moving to book-keeping. There were already spiteful tongues who would say how often they had seen Agnes in Ewan Fletcher's car, so it did not take much guessing to know how she had got herself considered for the job.

Agnes then talked to Ewan. He was not unaware of the obstacles, but suggested she should bring all her homework and class work related to mathematics and show his uncle, a sort of prelude to the interview. This she did. William Bourne talked to Mr. Green.

Ewan, full of ideas for innovation on the farm, was bold enough to say that women were coming into their own. Why not give Agnes a chance, for say six months?

Had Agnes overheard the arguments that followed she would have been embarrassed. She was not worth it; she was only the daughter of Bert Cooper. Ewan persisted. His uncle said he must be sweet on the girl. Ewan denied this and said there was too big an age gap for anything romantic, but he admired the fact that she was clever. She had stuck to her point when asking for ingredients for fudge, and William Bourne had to agree that he had been surprised at her polite boldness and maturity.

Finally he agreed to give her a chance. She could come as an office worker, perhaps leading to becoming a bookkeeper. There would be an office manager.

Agnes knew she would be making tea and at everyone's beck and call, for that was how women were treated, but she would be given a chance at book-keeping, confident that Ewan would see to that.

At family tea time again, Agnes told of her plans. Her parents just stared, for it was a world of which they knew nothing. They did not know if the words 'dual entry book-keeping was a real phrase or some sort of joke. Office matters were totally beyond their experience.

Dolly was supportive. She searched through their store of cast-off Taylor garments and from navy fabric made a straight skirt with a pleat at the back and a jacket long enough to reach well below the waist, a sort of copy of a man's suit. She also made blouses in white, beige and cream fabric. Each had a lacy frill at the neckline. It made Agnes look older than her years and gave her a competent air.

Agnes started work the following week. She loved her job, and yes, she made tea, but, working in the front office, she welcomed visitors, and was given a specific ledger related to corn sales. She was on her way to breaking into a whole new world, for herself, for her family and for women in general. Perhaps in cities women were in similar positions but she was breaking new ground in this rural area, that was for sure.

She began to wear less formal clothes to church. By the time she was sixteen Ewan was open about noticing her. He would come across after church and kiss her briefly on the cheek, then chat. He would have liked to see more of her and she would have welcomed any attention from him, though she admitted it to no one, not even Dolly. Unfortunately, Ewan was away a great deal and when he was at Oak Hill he spent a lot of time closeted with his uncle.

"Not got a fancy for him, has she?" her grandmother asked her daughter. "Fool if she has. He's just messing about. Way above her league. These young dandies with a bit of money. He'll not look seriously at her. You'd better warn her or your Agnes will get her heart broken."

This was not repeated to Agnes, though her mother did try probing Dolly about what was going on. Dolly could in all honesty say she had no idea. The two sisters were still close, still good friends, but they never talked to each other about their male friends, Ewan Fletcher and Peter Brunnick.

Agnes would keep her council, which was her way, but there was no doubt that she felt as May did. Just five minutes with Ewan was a treat, but how she wished he would stay and chat for longer when he was there after church.

Agnes did not go to the dances. She seemed content to spend her time off at home, which was surprising, since she had said she had no wish to stay at home on leaving school. The only change was that she would surreptitiously pick up a discarded newspaper and turn to any articles about finance.

Chapter 7

Dolly and May continued to go to the dances. Cyril left New Medic and went off to complete his training as a priest, but he came down to see May as often as he could. However, May had lost much of her sparkle. The music for the dancing was reduced to the services of a pianist, or they would dance to records. Even Peter was seen less.

Bert still worried about unemployment, but JFV, the Joint Farm Venture, flourished and he had no real grounds for his suspicions. It was a matter of everyone keeping their nerve and seeing what politicians would lead the country into.

May continued at Elliotts. She too would tell of the cars that were now appearing in their town, nudging for space on the streets among the horse-drawn vehicles. Occasionally a plane would be seen flying overhead, the pilot sometimes visible in his open cockpit.

The Taylor girls had their moment of glory at court

and 'came out'. They now relied less on Dolly, and often stayed in London, travelling up and down to town by train. They came back with tales of traffic jams, cars upsetting horse-drawn vehicles, noise, bustle and wonderful dress shops.

Then came the blow that everyone had feared. War with Germany was declared on 4th August 1914. By the end of September there were posters saying " Your country needs you." On each poster there was a picture of Kitchener pointing a finger. Excitement among the young men in towns and villages was hyped up by visiting officials. Recruitment offices opened in town centres at first, then one opened in Oak Hill. There was much nudging and daring among the young men, who encouraged each other to sign up.

Dolly could never understand how people could be led into believing what she saw as blatant lies. Yes, the army may mean three meals a day and a uniform and good boots to wear but at the end it usually meant... She could not face the thought.

Mothers worrying about what the neighbours thought would say put on a show of supporting the cause. "My son's as brave as yours," said one woman as she pushed her seventeen-year-old into the queue. There was no turning back once a signature was on the form. Johnny Markham and his older brother James, both of whom May and Dolly knew, signed up, as did Donald Booker.

Their train left one Saturday afternoon and May and Dolly went to wave them off.

Within weeks those young men were fighting at the Battle of the Somme.

Many were the gloomy days when Bert and Dolly stood leaning over the garden fence after reading the list of missing or dead. There were endless columns of names. Prayers in church focused on war and each week there were middle-aged or old men and women in the congregation who were looking pale and had clearly been crying. It was not unknown for a sob to break out and echo round the church.

Agnes and Dolly silently gave thanks that as yet their brothers were too young to fight.

Rumours of those who had fallen spread around the village, but Dolly and her father checked details in the national and local press before making any comment. They heard that Johnny Markham had been killed, and one Thursday his name was in both the local and national newspaper in the lists of the dead. Dolly went to see May and they agreed that they had to visit Johnny's parents, but perhaps it would be hard if they both turned up together, so Dolly went on the Friday and May, with Cyril, on the Saturday. Mr and Mrs Markham were touched by their sympathy and said support from Johnny's young friends really did help. They liked to talk about their son and to learn how well liked he had been.

That Sunday a loud sob from Mr. Markham echoed round the church as the vicar led prayers for the dead, missing and wounded. Handkerchiefs came out and both men and women were clearly upset by the sound of a man in church crying. Why did everyone think men should not cry?

After the service Dolly went to sit on the seat on the north side of the church, looking, as in a trance, at the old tombstones there. She was in a raw state emotionally, and that was the only excuse she could give to herself later for the spiteful words that would soon tumble unbidden from her mouth. She did not really think enlisting was essential, stupid, in fact, as it led to so much loss of life, but that was not what she thought at that moment. She felt that everyone who could enlist should, to get revenge for the death of Johnny and others from their own country. That was the patriotic and essential thing to do. Anger boiled within her. She had no time for any man who was either not in the armed forces nor about to join.

Just then she saw Peter come round the corner. She was thrilled to see him. He came up to her, touched her hand briefly and smiled into her eyes, saying, 'Hello'. They sat together. They might wander round the village later but they had not been 'walking out' long. It was too soon to use the lonely field paths.

They were at ease together, until their chat turned to the Great War.

"My cousin Elmer is off on Thursday," he told her in a level voice. "He has joined the Glorious Glosters."

" When will you be going, Peter? It may be brassy of me because we've not known each other long, but I shall miss you, you know."

She took his hand and squeezed it. Thinking of those who had already signed up and the news from The Somme, her eyes filled with tears.

"Me? I'm not going."

Perhaps it was the build up from the last few days that made the words burst from her. She spoke quickly and the pitch of her voice changed as she said in anger, "Not going? But you have to. It's up to everyone to do their bit. You're not, you're not a consc..." Her voice gagged and she could not get the words 'conscientious objector' out.

"Haven't you heard what Kitchener is saying? Your country needs you. Oh Peter. I don't want you to go, but..." Again she could not finish the sentence. She was thinking, *What will the neighbours think if I walk out with a coward?*

She went on determinedly.

"I think there will be conscription soon. Our neighbour, Millie, cries every night because her Frank has joined up, but she is so proud of him. I'd feel the same about you, Peter. You work in an office, so it's not a job that keeps you here, is it? Won't your relatives be resentful if you stay home while others in the family are at the front?"

"Dolly, let me explain," he began.

She closed her eyes and took a deep breath.

"I think I love you Peter, yes already, different as we are. Just looking at you makes my heart beat faster. I'm sure I'm not understanding. You're not going yet, is that what you mean?"

Peter, unknown to her, had already had to deal with criticism of cowardice and she had hit a raw spot. At her words he felt as though his heart had broken in two, but it also angered him.

He stood up. "I shall not justify myself to you, Dolly, nor to anyone else. I have thought about you ever since we met. Sundays could not come quickly enough for me to see you again. But I will not be challenged."

He put on his cap and walked away. As he walked out of her sight he began to wheeze; the asthma returning. By heaven, if only he could join up, he thought. He would make her proud of him.

Dolly knew nothing of Peter's asthma. As she stood up to set off home, Dolly was troubled. How could he not be enlisting? He must feel guilty or he would not have taken the hump like that. What should she have said? Not once did she think she should have put her arms round him and held on tight, thankful that she would still have her man with her.

Ewan was in church one Sunday, only a couple of weeks after that. He came across to Agnes. He did not touch her or smile but said in a low voice, "Come for a drive with me Agnes, this afternoon. I'll pick you up about two."

"I'll wait here, by the lychgate," said Alice. "Half past two would be better. I'll have to be home for Sunday lunch. Mum makes such an effort."

Agnes dressed with care and took with her a floppy hat and a wispy, pink scarf with which to tie it on. As she went through the kitchen Dolly caught her eye and raised her eyebrows. Agnes did not stop to explain. She was glad Dolly was the only one who had noticed her as she left.

Agnes was first by the church gate. Ewan drew up in his car and got out to help her climb in, which he had never done before. "You look very pretty today, Agnes," he said. Once he was back in the driver's seat he leant across and touched her shoulder. As she looked at him he merely said, "Tie your hat on tight."

They drove out to a spot where there was a distant view across farmland. They could see the Malvern Hills in the distance, shrouded in grey and brown hues and undulating across the skyline.

Ewan switched off his engine and sat for a moment staring ahead.

"I wanted to join the Royal Flying Corps."

"What do you mean, wanted?"

"Last week you did an impressive job greeting our MP

and the government official with him. You made quite an impression. Well done, Agnes."

She waited. He had not driven here just to say that. She wondered why he had ignored her question.

He gave a deep sigh. "I had planned to join up, do my bit, but it seems I am needed elsewhere. Look ahead Agnes, Isn't that a sight? Acres and acres of farmland, all loved and cared for by men of the land, men whose parents and grandparents worked those acres before them. It's a wonder. Horses are going to continue to be of great importance, but many are going to be used by the army abroad. I think there are plans for the government to supply us with some tractors.

"Farming is there to feed us all. It seems I am needed to go from farm to farm and guide them on how to make the best use of what we have. Men who know those things are leaving the land and signing up. Uncle William working with other farms is seen as the best option, and I am to be the lead. I'll be talking others into forming farming co-ops. Tell them what can be done. It's a government job, so I shall be a civilian. I suppose I shouldn't mind. In a strange way I shall be doing it for my country, and our people have to be fed. I shall get a vehicle and travel all over the place. It's not what I want, Agnes. It's what I must do."

Agnes felt the chill tension in the air.

"Will it be a posh car, Ewan?" she asked, trying to lighten the chat.

"A van, if I choose. No farmer will welcome me if I turn up looking flash. A van would make me more acceptable, and I hope once I am known they'll get used to the idea of listening to the 'government man'." Thanks for coming out today, Agnes. I wanted you to know. I am not a coward. I have to do my bit, but in a different way. I shall not be in Oak Hill much. I shall miss you." He touched her shoulder lightly. "By the time I get back you'll be head book-keeper and Uncle William will be doing exactly as you tell him". He turned and smiled as he said it.

He started the engine and they drove back. He dropped her at the church gate, sounded his blaring horn and was gone.

That night Dolly went into the bedroom to find Agnes with her hand on the button hook. She jumped as Dolly came in.

"Sorry for touching your things."

"You're welcome, you know that. Is everything all right, Agnes?"

"Its all strange. I don't like it. I can't cope, but I suppose I have to. Yes. I guess I'm all right, sort of."

Agnes was then nearly seventeen. She went downstairs to make the inevitable pot of tea for everyone.

Dancing seemed sacrilege with so much gloom around.

The fortnightly hops were to close. At the final dance women danced with women, there being few young men left in the village now.

If there was a silver lining, it was that Agnes's job was secure. With so many men at the front, she was needed here.

Bert could have stopped worrying too, for there was a shortage of labour for the farm and women were now seen in the fields at all seasons, not just at harvest. But he continued to worry anyway. It fitted in with the air of gloom that was around.

Julia Taylor's viscount joined up, becoming an officer in a guards regiment. Julia went to become a nurse in a stately home in Berkshire which had been requisitioned as a military hospital.

The indoor and outdoor staff at the Taylors' home were now sadly depleted. Some of the rooms were shut up and visitors did not come. Dolly felt that she was now kicking her heels with not enough to do, but what were her options? She had now been a housemaid for some time. She grew critical, irrationally so. An event or an item of news would catch her on the raw. She resented the young men she still saw around and wondered why they had not signed up.

She was ready to gripe to May about Cyril, because he was safe in Birmingham. He had joined up and was an army officer and a padre. He had got the posting he wanted and was soon administering to newly wounded men who arrived at the hospital where he was based, shell shocked, some blind, some with limbs missing, many gassed in the trenches. He also worked with the mentally ill.

He worked with families of conscientious objectors, for they were badly treated by the populace, being shouted at or spat on in the streets for harbouring cowards. Dolly began to understand there were reasons for people's actions, and it was not all as black and white as she had once been sure it was.

May continued at Elliotts, Agnes at Bourne's and Dolly at Taylors. They were all restless, and this had something to do with the tedium of life, for recreational activities had ceased and after work each of them went home to kick her heels and wonder what tomorrow would bring.

Chapter 8

The war had been raging for over two years when Dolly saw a story in the paper about lathe workers, complete with a picture. The job looked interesting. She asked around and wondered about applying. Teatime was still the best time in the Cooper household to make announcements, and so, having reached a decision, that was when she decided to make her announcement.

"Dad," Dolly called out as she went up the path.

"Here. You're early," said Bert as he came out of his shed.

"No. Usual time, but I'm going to say something important after tea and I want your support."

"That sounds ominous. You're not going to cause ructions, are you? If you are, let me eat my tea first. You know what your mother is like when she gets in a mood."

"But I want you to be on my side, Dad. I'm going to leave domestic service at Taylor's and go to the factory at

Merricks. They're advertising for lathe workers, women in particular."

Her father stared. By then they were through the back door. Dolly's three young brothers were at the table and her sister was making a pot of tea.

They were just about finishing the meal when Dolly said in a loud voice, "I'm leaving Taylors. I'm after a job at Merricks as a lathe worker."

There was silence for a moment. Then her mother said, "You're what? I think not, my girl. Whoever heard of a woman in a factory? That is no job for a woman."

Of course women had worked in factories, mill workers in the cotton industry for starters, but not in these parts. Dolly knew it, but she also knew this was not a good time to correct her mother, who perhaps was right anyway about this particular kind of factory.

In a gentle, reasonable voice, Dolly replied, "The men are off fighting the Kaiser. Lots of women are going into factories."

In chorus her brothers chanted noisily, "England's sure to win the war, We'll get a treacle tin and put the Kaiser in, And he won't see his mammy any more."

Their mother clipped the closest one round the ear.

"Not now boys," said their father. "If you've finished, go off and play. Half an hour till bedtime mind, and come when your mother calls you."

With them out of the way, the talk continued.

"What about the night shifts?" asked her mother.

"Early shift and late," answered Dolly. "No nights, not for women. Seven in the morning till three, or three in the afternoon till eleven in the evening. Only thing is, five days on, one off, so I'll work on Sundays. The factory never closes."

"Will you be the only woman working there?" asked her dad.

"No. Enid Watts is there for a start. "

"That strumpet," said her Dad scornfully.

"There are others there too."

There was a brief silence, then Beattie said, "To think that my daughter…"

"Our," Bert cut in. "Our daughter. She's mine too." This seemed to spur him on, for he got up and walked round the table, stopping behind his wife's chair. He put his hands on her shoulders, squeezed them then bent and kissed her on the cheek.

"Our daughter is clever, and by heck she's got plenty of spunk. I think she gets it from you, Beattie. It's why I married you." Again he bent and kissed his wife on the cheek, then went back and sat down. "There's one bit of good that will come out of this great war, as far as I can see," he went on. "If anything good does come out of a war, it's that women's input will be valued and opportunities will open up for them. No job for a woman? Think of our Agnes. It started with the suffragettes and by gum I hope it continues. I for one support it."

Beattie drew in her breath but before another tirade could follow, Agnes got up and said calmly, "Shall I make a fresh pot of tea?"

So Dolly got a job in the factory making parts for tanks and armaments. It was dark, noisy and smelly, the smell being a mixture of grease and swarf, the metallic dust shaved by the machines. There was a light over each machine, but nowhere else, and the noise of all the machines up and running at once seemed unbearable for the first day, but she got used to it. Training was minimal, and in the first half hour she learned that turnround must be swift and accurate. Failure and you were out. She kept up with and in some cases outstripped the output of some of the men, but as a woman her wage was less per hour than men earned, and it would ever be so.

There was much ribaldry from the male workers, particularly the older ones. She soon learned it was best to ignore their jibes. She also learned to step niftily beside her machine at the right moments to avoid having her backside pinched.

"Coming out with me then?" someone would call out and she would say "Yeah, but not tonight." It was not long before the men knew she could give as good as she got. She parried lewd suggestions from married men. They soon learned that she was no pushover, and they began to accept her and chat to her in friendly manner when arriving and leaving. There was little time for chat whilst they were actually working and it was difficult to hear what was said when all the machines were running.

She kept a smile and, love it or hate it, she did not complain to the bosses and before long was accepted. She certainly pulled her weight.

At times she would get a sincere invitation to 'walk out' with a bachelor, but she never accepted. The men were nice enough, but always the face of Peter Brunnick passed before her eyes. If there was a knees -up, say at Christmas, she joined in and laughed and sang with the best, but when she danced she disliked the feel of a man's arm round her waist and wanted it to be Peter's. Yet she heard nothing from him. There was no reason why she should, after the way they had parted.

Agnes seemed calm and unassuming, working hard and daily gaining the respect of William Bourne, but she missed Ewan Fletcher. His visits to Oak Hill were brief and months could go by when she did not see him on the farm. When he did appear it would be a quick 'Hello', then he would be closeted with his uncle and soon he would be gone again.

For two more years the war dragged on until finally, on November 11th 1918, the Armistice was signed. Great was the excitement across the country, and in Oak Hill. There were flags everywhere. Many small Union Jacks were poked into hedges by front doors, while bigger ones hung from lamp-posts. Men having a beer to celebrate overflowed from the bars at both The Fox and The Royal Oak onto the paths. The killing had continued even on November 10th, but now it was over, done with, there would be no wars ever again, or so people chose to believe. There was laughing, singing and dancing in houses in the village, and the Coopers set out to make theirs the noisiest in the lane. It was a day never to be forgotten.

Three days later, on 14th November, Bert was crossing the yard at work when Ewan appeared.

"Mr. Cooper!" he called out.

Here it comes, thought Bert. Now the war was over, the blighter couldn't wait till the end of the week to get rid of him. Mr. Cooper, not Bert – that was warning enough. No doubt he was about to be chucked out. He had warned Dolly ages ago, and now it had come.

Ewan walked up to Bert. An onlooker watching them as they talked would have said it was Ewan who was up tight, not Bert. After a brief chat Bert straightened his cap and the two men shook hands. Bert wiped the back of his hand across his mouth and left the yard whistling tunelessly between his teeth, heading for home. He seemed to be smiling.

Agnes was the last to get home for tea. Dolly asked her, "Agnes, can you give me a hand for a bit? That dress I altered for you. The shell pink one with the lace and silk ruffle. I want to copy it but can't remember just how I did it. If you would come upstairs and try it on, I'll get my beige one out and get it sorted."

"What about Mum and tea?"

"I'll manage," said Beattie, "and anyway we may be eating a bit late. Your father wants to say something to the boys."

Up in the bedroom Dolly took off her dress and stood in her petticoat. She picked up a handful of pins.

"What've they been up to now?" asked Agnes.

"Dunno. Come on Agnes, put the dress on." Agnes pulled on the as yet unworn shell pink frock. Dolly moved behind her and stretched up to take the hairpins out of Agnes's hair so that it fell round her shoulders.

"What are you doing?"

"Just letting your hair down. You look so strait-laced in your work clothes. You scare me. There, that's better." She flicked the hair away from Agnes's face so it hung down her back.

Bert shouted up the stairs, "One of you girls. There's someone at the back door. Answer it."

"You go, Dolly."

"In my petticoat and with a hand full of pins? You'll have to go, Agnes."

"Door!" shouted Bert again. The girls were not in the way of defying their father, so down went Agnes to open the back door. Her parents stood by the kitchen table,

Bert holding down young Jim, who had evidently been trying to get up and answer the door. No one spoke. They all looked solemn.

Agnes opened the door. In stepped Ewan.

"Ewan!"

"Agnes. You were pretty when you were fourteen and I first saw you. Now you are beautiful, stunningly beautiful. How old are you now?"

"Twenty."

"And I'm an old man of twenty-eight."

Bert firmly closed the door between scullery and kitchen.

"What's going on?" asked Jim.

"Shh" said everyone, including Dolly, who had come into the room fully clothed.

It was not long before Agnes and Ewan came into the kitchen holding hands, Agnes looking very flushed and very flustered. Ewan held tight to Agnes but shook Bert's hand, then turned to shake Beattie's saying, "Mrs. Cooper."

It was Beattie who made a pot of tea. Dolly wondered how the happy couple would drink theirs, as they seemed reluctant to let go of each other.

Ewan was keen to sit with the Cooper family in church the next Sunday but wanted Agnes to have an engagement ring by then. He had toyed with the idea of taking her to London to buy one, but knew she had never been there, and he wanted the day to stand out in her mind as the day they got the ring and not have it overshadowed.

In the local town was an Italian jeweller. He sold quality goods, not cheap but of solid worth. On the Saturday they stood outside Boretti's.

"Had you anything particular in mind?" he asked.

Agnes hesitated then said, "Something different, not the usual solitaire or half hoop of gem stones."

Ewan had made a preliminary visit and a tray of emerald rings was brought out. Agnes was immediately taken by a long rectangular emerald flanked by a single diamond on each side, each diamond encircled by a ring of gold. She tried it on. Many a girl could not have carried it off, but she had long, slender fingers and the ring sat well on them. The decision was made.

She wandered round the shop while he paid. He put the ring in its box in his pocket. They drove out to the countryside, to the viewpoint where he had once told her about wanting to join the Royal Flying Corps, then got out of the car and leaned against the radiator. The view was now different, for some fields were bare and a rich brown after ploughing. In some there was a fawn hue where the stubble had yet to be cleared. The grass on others was still green, and the shape and colour of the Malvern Hills in the distance were unchanged.

He turned to her.

"I'm glad you agreed on an emerald. I see it as a colour

of the countryside. We are both from farming stock, you and me. Both my grandfathers were tenant farmers.

Yes, I have been privileged, thanks mostly to Uncle William, and you have most certainly grown up with farming."

He took out the ring and spread her fingers across the palm of his hand. He slid it on to her finger and looked down at her. Then he pointed first to one diamond then the other.

"These sparkle like the stars in your eyes, Agnes. I fell in love with you when you were fourteen. You were laughing and your eyes sparkled. A number of infants were staring in awe at my tractor. Then, when I saw you outside the school and you were crying because some of those children had had no dinner I wanted to put my arms round you. There has never been anyone else, ever."

He let go of her hand to embrace her, then bent to kiss her.

It was some time later that he released his hold, but still too soon in her mind. They got back into the car to drive back to Oak Hill.

Chapter 9

On a Friday three years later, Mr. Merrick called Dolly into his office at the factory.

"Dolly, you're a good worker and you've been here a long time – what is it, five years or thereabouts? I wanted to say that before I begin. And also, your job is safe, for the moment. But now men are coming here asking for work, men who have served their country. It's getting nasty, Dolly. I turn them away and only last night as I left the factory three were hanging about by the gates and I got shouted at.

"I am employing a woman, but there are men who could do the job, your job."

"Are orders not coming in?" she asked.

"No, it's not that," he said. "Now we're making parts for cars and, keep it to yourself for now, I've just landed a big order for parts for those steam engines that are pulling ploughs across fields. Had to go to Leeds to get it. A man and horse plough an acre a day. These new set-ups can do twenty acres a day. I pride myself that I can wheedle an order out of anyone. No, it's not lack of work."

"So what is it?" she asked.

"Out of work men think women should go back to the kitchen and men should work machines, like your machine, your lathe. They think it's no job for a woman in peace time when men are out of work. Strikes are threatened. I'll keep you on while I can, but..." He shrugged.

Dolly's shoulders sagged.

"There used to be lots of banter here," she said. "I could cope with that and I got used to stepping aside and dodging a pinch on the backside. I could laugh it off, Mr Merrick, but now they don't talk to me. Thay walk the other side of a machine, to avoid me."

"Well Dolly, it's their neighbours and relatives who come here asking for work. A rowdy bunch of them came to talk about it. They are between the devil and the hard stuff Dolly, nothing against you exactly but that's how it is. I thought it only right to warn you."

Dolly said nothing at home about this discussion.

On the Sunday there was to be a special church service beginning at ten, one hour earlier than usual. May was back with Cyril, and a now heavily pregnant Agnes was coming over with Ewan for the day.

Beattie, wishing to see Dolly settled and knowing nothing about the trouble at Merrick's, brought up the old chestnut again while they were washing up the breakfast things.

"You should get married, Dolly. There's still Percy Wilkins."

"No!"

"Well you may as well..."

"I will not be marrying Percy Wilkins, and that is final."

She left the room to get ready for church.

The large war memorial the village was planning was not ready, but a plaque was up in the church listing those from the village who had died in the Great War. The local stonemason was amongst the dead but one of his erstwhile apprentices had carved the plaque and made a fair job of it.

When they got to the church, it was packed. At the end of the service there was the usual chit chat, which Dolly joined, but then she doubled back and stood looking at the plaque.

She sensed that someone was behind her, but she did not turn round.

"Did you know them?" It was a deep , cultured voice.

"Yes." She leaned forward and put her fingers on one name. "Private M. Fielding. I didn't know him. I think he was staying in the village and signed up from here, but he wasn't from these parts."

She ran her fingers over another name, Pte J. Markham.

"I started school the same day as Johnny Markham," she said.

She moved on. Captain C. Hollis.

"He was the eldest son of Lord Hollis, our local nob. It took men indiscriminately, the war. So many lost, so much sorrow."

She turned to leave, then took a step back in surprise. The man was Peter Brunnick.

"Remember me?" he said. "How are you, Dolly? Is that seat still on the north side of the church? Come and talk to me for a little while, Dolly, please."

Once seated they turned to face each other.

"You look well, Peter. You are a much better colour."

Peter smiled. "So you do remember me. You look perfect, Dolly. Pale blue was always your colour and today you are perfect. You've had your hair cut." He leaned forward to touch a dark curl that was peeping out from under her fashionable hat. She should have drawn back. It was not at all the thing for a man one had not seen for several years to do, but instead she smiled.

"Thank you. You are very kind."

"No Dolly, I am not kind. I am blown away by you, as I always was. I say what is true." He paused. "We did not part on good terms."

Silence followed, but neither moved. Dolly spoke first.

"You lost some of your friends. The poets. Dad and I read about them in the paper. Rupert Brooke's poem with the line *In some corner of a foreign field* was in Dad's paper. I thought of you when I read it."

"Did you, Dolly? I'm glad, glad you thought of me. Not glad about Rupert Brooke of course."

"I never did get to read Hardy. *Hodge the Drummer boy*. Had I stayed with Taylors they might have had a copy in their library. Last time I saw Alexandra things were bad. Strange how war changes things that looked as if they would last for ever. Old Sir Andrew Taylor had a stroke. Alexandra is trying to run the place but it looks so neglected. I felt sorry for her. They still have a special pew in church, but life is hard for Alexandra. I don't know why I am telling you this, but you were always a good listener, Peter. Tell me about yourself. How have you been?"

He edged closer and took her hand.

"A bit more about you first." He touch the ring finger on her left hand.

"No ring. So you are not married. I was determined to see you again. If you had been in church with a tall handsome husband and five little children clinging to your skirts I would have gone away with the image of you in my mind stored away for ever. I had to see you, even if it was for the last time."

There was a pause, then he went on, "You left Taylor's?" He did not let go of her hand.

"Yes, I work in a factory. I work on a machine, a lathe."

"Gone up in the world then." He smiled as he said it.

"Not if my mother is to be believed. She thinks only sl… well, she thinks nice women do not work in factories. If she's asked she says I used to work for Sir Andrew Taylor and she doesn't say what I do now. Daft, isn't it? Everyone here knows everyone's business anyway, but she still worries about what the neighbours think. Your turn, Peter."

"I left the flour mill. My father had to accept it. He came to understand. It will be mine one day, as will the farm."

"Do you have any brothers? Do they work with your dad?"

"No, there's just Dad and me. That's why it was hard for him to see why I had to leave the mill. He saw it as letting him down, but he's getting used to the idea. I live in a cottage in Dymock, in the Forest of Dean. He comes to see me now. I'm outside a lot. No more cigarette smoke in a stuffy office or dust from the mill. I could beat you at croquet, though probably not at tennis." He squeezed her hand and laughed. "It's being outside that's made the difference. Fresh air suits me. As for a job, I'm a reporter for the Forest News. I'm a writer in my spare time." Teasingly he added, "I could write a book about you. I'd call it 'Girl on a Lathe'."

"I hope there will be a chapter about how the women who kept this country afloat during the war are being treated now," she replied sharply with bitterness in her voice.

He went on. He had come with an agenda, meaning to seek her out and, if she was still single, put her in the picture about himself.

"I've just inherited Waverley. Lots of business meetings this past week about that."

"You own Waverley? Does that make you lord of the croquet lawn?" She resorted to teasing as she could not think what else to say.

He laughed. "No titles in our family. What should it be, if I had a title that is?"

"Lord Mallet, because of the croquet."

They laughed together.

"We were always on the same wavelength, Dolly. It's good to be here with you and to laugh together. What should the lady of Waverley be called?"

"Is there one?"

"No Dolly. I am not married. This is just nonsense to make us laugh. Lady Mallet perhaps?"

"Something that sounds more grand. Chatelaine of the croquet lawn. How's that?"

Again they laughed together, but her heart sank. Did

he have a future wife lined up? How she wished she was that lucky woman.

"So you'll be moving to Waverley? That's nice."

"I want to stay in Dymock, keep doing the job I do now. I don't know yet what to do about Waverley. Let it out perhaps."

She kept quiet.

"Come on Dolly, tell me what you're thinking."

She just smiled and said nothing.

"Dolly?"

"Well, it will cost a lot to run Waverley. Can you do that on a reporter's wage?"

"This is between us, Dolly. I don't need to work. A hefty sum came with Waverley, but I should hate to see it empty, unloved, uncared for. Something philanthropic would be good. Convalescent home for ex- military personnel, something like that. It's early days. Let's leave it for now. Tell me the gossip from Oak Hill. How's your family?"

"Will is working and courting. Different girl every night of the week, if our dad is to be believed. Lenny has a job too, and Jim is all set to join Dad on the farm. It's strange in a way. Our Agnes married Ewan Fletcher, so Dad works for his son-in-law and Jim will be working for his brother-in-law. Wiiliam Bourne is still owner, but Ewan runs the place and JFV is going strong."

Time was getting on and Peter wanted to get to what he had really come to say.

"That last meeting, do you still hate me for not joining up? I never did, you know."

Just then Bert appeared round the corner. "We're just off home, our Dolly."

"I'll be along in a minute," she said. Bert and Peter looked at each other.

"Mr Brunnick!" said Bert. "What a change. How are you, young man?"

Peter jumped up and the two men shook hands then put an arm round each other to thump each other on the back. They stood apart.

"I have much to thank you for, Bert. In fact everything to thank you for. I owe you my life."

Bert turned to Dolly. "Years ago I found this young man lying in a patch of brambles by the field path just outside the churchyard. He was red in the face. His chest was swollen and he was gasping for breath. I knew it was asthma, but I've never seen an attack like it. I thought he was a goner. I ran back to the church and fortunately the vicar was still there. We trundled the bier, you know the cart they put coffins on, down as close to him as we could and hoisted him on. It seemed he'd had a thumping great row with the love of his life. He kept saying, 'I wanted to join up but they wouldn't have me. They wouldn't have me'. We pushed him back as far as the church porch and the vicar rushed off to get the doctor."

"And they saved me." There were tears in Peter's eyes as he again thanked Bert.

"I'm not sure you wanted to be saved, not then at any rate."

"I didn't. I lay on that bier and wished I was in my coffin and my awful, awful life was over."

"And now?" asked Bert.

"I'm well and I'm enjoying life, thanks to you and the vicar."

"Come home and meet my wife," said Bert. "She'd love to meet you."

"Does Mum know about this?" asked Dolly.

"No, our Dolly, the vicar and I agreed that we would tell no one for this young man might one day want to hold his head up and his misery was best left behind him."

"Our Dolly?" Peter queried.

"This is my father."

"Small world," they said in unison. All three laughed. Peter put his arm round Dolly's shoulders and gave her a squeeze.

The two men turned to walk to the lychgate. Dolly turned to go the other way.

"I'll catch you up," called Peter to Bert. He ran back and grabbed Dolly's arm.

"And where do you think you are going, Love of my life?"

"I'm so ashamed, Peter, ashamed of myself. I can never make amends."

"Oh yes you can. You owe me, young woman, and you should feel obliged to take me to your home and make me welcome."

"Wouldn't that be a sort of blackmail to make me go with you?"

"Probably, but if it gets you by my side I shall consider it all worth it. It's what I came here for."

He took her hand and held on tight. They ran to catch up with her dad.

Back at the house, everyone seemed to be trying to talk at once. The story was told. Peter and Ewan hit it off straight away, and there was much laughter.

After lunch voices quietened, everyone feeling stuffed and relaxed. Bert leant back in his chair with his eyes almost closed. He was not asleep, but was looking round at his family and thinking about each of them in turn.

Agnes, as a child had seemed so quiet, and now she was living in the big house, for William Bourne had moved to a smaller place and Ewan and Agnes had moved into the main property. 'Yes Mrs. Fletcher. No Mrs. Fletcher,' Bert heard people say respectfully to her. Who would have thought it?

Will.. Everyone liked Will. He fooled about and was

full of blarney, but he knew where he was heading. He was a salesman, selling tractors, of all things, but he knew all about them and had talked many a tight-fisted farmer into parting with his cash. He suited the job and the job suited him.

Lenny was not happy. He had got a job in a racing stable but, truth be told, he was scared of the horses. One had grabbed his cap as he passed the stable door and he had come home in a mood. Bert had laughed out loud, which had not helped. He knew Lenny was asking Dolly if there were any jobs going at Merrick's. Yes, he and Beattie worried about Lenny. Of all his children only Jim was interested in farming. He'd start work soon.

Dolly was the first and last to fill his thoughts, as ever. She had got a posh twang to her voice while working for Taylor's, and had never lost it. She still had the button hook but had collected no other treasures, either sentimental or of value. Beattie had feared she would grow coarse, for that was how she viewed factory workers, but Dolly seemed to be able to be two people at once, the posh daughter at home, but ordinary in the workplace, or so he heard.

He had had ideas of how she would turn out, but it had not happened. She kept her thoughts to herself and led a rather dull life. It was as though she was seeking something, wanting something that had not come her way. He could not make her out. Although they still had their private chats, she gave nothing away. Fate is strange. He had had such hopes for her.

Suddenly Agnes bent double and shouted, "Owwww!" then groaned. Beattie took charge, sent Bert off to get the midwife and ushered Agnes upstairs. Ewan went into a cold sweat and got in everyone's way. You would think he was the one about to give birth. Peter took him outside and spent the next two hours walking up and down the garden with him. Ewan refused to go further than the front gate.

The wait seemed to go on for ever, but at last the cry of a new baby was heard. Ewan rushed upstairs to be with his wife, then came down to say it was a boy. They were going to name him Peter William, the first name after himself and the second after the baby's great uncle. He then dashed back upstairs.

Bert took the boys into his shed to unearth a hidden crate of beer so that they could celebrate becoming uncles. He was not sure he was celebrating himself, for he did not know how he felt about being a granddad. That was a name for old men.

Peter took Dolly's hand and led her into the front room. He sat on an armchair and pulled her down onto his knee.

"It occurs to me that the newly arrived Peter William will need some cousins to play with when he comes to see his Cooper grandparents, cousins who have come over from the Forest of Dean," he said. "I think I think it is up to you and me to provide them, three or four at least." He brushed a wisp of hair from her forehead and tenderly ran a finger down her cheek. This gentle, caring man, the man Dolly had dreamed of for years. For her, since the moment he had first spoken to her outside the church, there had never had been any other. When he had walked her home from the village dances she had wished he could be all over her as Cyril had been with May, but he had kept his distance. Now she could feel his breath on her cheek as he pulled her close and asked, "So what's it to be, love of my life? Will you marry me?"

Bluebells

By P. Brunnick, reporter and poet
Inspired by the Forest of Dean in spring

Hush, tread softly through the woodland
Let no footfall sound be heard
Feel the peace that's here created
Disturb it not with human word.

Lightly move among the bluebells
Listen - you will hear them ring
A myriad, million blue heads nodding
Salvation for the soul they bring.

Admire their colour, tinged with purple,
as the evening shade draws on
Each is wistful, gently shaking
Creation's youth is in their throng.

Look not towards the treetops mighty
of oaks mature that hide the cloud,
where squawking birds disturb the stillness
or branches make invasive sound

Transparent wings divide these kingdoms,
all unseen by human eye
and as they quiver, so the bluebells
wave their heads, then you and I

Trusting in God-given senses,
await the joy the flowers bring,
in the aura of the woodland
to hear a million bluebells ring.